REVELATION

the return of

Mr. Breeze

Morrie Richfield

ISBN: 0615736467
ISBN-13: 9780615736464

This book is dedicated to my friend, Suni, who passed away in my arms on March 30, 2012. From her, I learned how to love.

And to Michele Frank, who gave me a reason to want to love again.

Chapter One

Wednesday, May 2, 2012

––––––––

Yes, it is me, Michael Ryan. I'm sure you remember me. After all, for a short time, I was about the most famous man in the world. For those of you who have forgotten, let me fill you in on what has happened in the two years since I last saw Zackary Breeze and Rover.

Of course you must remember Zack Breeze and Rover. Zack as he called himself is this time is our maker. He cured our diseases told us our religions are nothing but of our own making and turned a normal German Sheppard dog whose name is Rover into the second most powerful being on the planet. Let's not forget that he used me to write his story and threatened our immediate destruction should I refuse.

I wrote the book that Zack asked me to write. It sold more copies than any book in history, and you all read it. I was oh so pleased with myself. I was rich, famous, and revered. You could not open a newspaper or magazine without seeing my name in it somewhere. It was my fifteen minutes of fame, so to speak.

For a time, there seemed to be hope in the world. The wars and fighting stopped—it was as if no one knew if the next shot fired would be the one that would bring the human race to an end. People seemed to like that I was somehow partly responsible for all of these remarkable things that had happened. I was admired by many, but what I did not know at the time was that I was hated by an equal number.

It seemed that once people heard Zack's words, most of them stopped going to churches, synagogues, mosques, or any public place of worship. They prayed on their front yards and in alleys and at any time they felt the need. Only now, they prayed to Zack, and a somewhat zealous few even prayed to me.

For those fanatics, you see, I was the messenger of God. Through me, they thought they could find salvation, and, boy, did they try. They camped out on my street, in my yard, and even in my neighbors' yards. They also built structures to honor me out of stuff from my trash and the trash of everyone else on the street. As you can probably imagine, my neighbors were not pleased, and neither was I. I was like a movie star; I couldn't go out in public without paparazzi on my tail and people asking me to touch them. My fifteen minutes of fame had turned into twenty-four hours a day of hell.

Then the reaction from the religious community came. They finally realized that without worshippers and money, they would not survive. For them, Zack meant the end of their existence, and I became their target for retaliation.

"The devil comes to us in many forms" became their rallying cry, and as for me, I became the devil's minion. I guess I couldn't blame them for trying to bring their followers back, but I was astounded by how many people believed them. They quickly forgot what they had seen and what Zack had done. They even managed to convince the majority of the world that Zack cured all of their diseases just so he could fool them into thinking he was our maker.

Let's also not forget how the pharmaceutical companies chimed in. After all, no more diseases meant no one needed medication, so no more business. They jumped right on that bandwagon and within a few months had almost everyone believing their miraculous cures were temporary. So back on the drugs they went, and back came the profits.

I suppose I should have expected there would be some reaction; after all, I always believed religion was nothing more than a very profitable business whose main currency was either hope or fear. If they could not get your money by making you believe in one, they would threaten you with the other. Just like any other business, they needed their customers to survive.

Suddenly, my home, my yard, and my street became the focal point for the battle between those who thought Zack was our savior and those who thought he was the devil. It was not a pretty sight. At first, there were just signs and lots of chanting, but then came the physical confrontations followed by the police in riot gear. I was a prisoner in my own house—that is, until someone decided to throw a Molotov cocktail through one of my windows and burn my house down.

I barely made it out in one piece, but the fire and the confusion surrounding it gave me a chance to get away without anyone noticing me. At first, they thought I had died in the fire, and the celebrations that ensued over that news were televised a bit too often for my liking. So I decided it was time to keep a very low profile.

That was how I ended up here in northwest Maryland, in a house my old friend Al had rented for me. I still had a few friends left, though most of them would rather I not mention their names.

I'd been living in this house on this quiet street for almost a year. At first, I tried to write, but I just couldn't find the words. Instead, I settled into a somewhat boring and mundane existence. Then, I had the brilliant idea that smoking pot and listening to the Grateful Dead might help me make some sense out of all this. So I called on another person I could still call a friend and asked him to send me up a whole bunch of it.

If the UPS driver only knew what she was delivering that day!

Oh, I'm sorry I forgot to tell you about Julie. You remember her; she was the woman I was with when all this started. She was not that thrilled with what Zack had made me realize about myself and was gone about thirty seconds after I was released from the hospital.

I suppose you could say that in many ways, I was living like a recluse. I had my food delivered, and I had not shaved or had a haircut in months. At first, I did it with the hope that it would make it harder for anyone to recognize me, but after a while, I kind of liked the look.

It seemed to fit my new lifestyle and made me feel more authentic as I got high all day with the Dead's music as my only companion.

My only other activity was looking out of my front windows. The house I was renting was a Cape Cod. It had a porch and big vertical windows across the front. It allowed me to see the comings and goings on the street. It also allowed me to see *her*.

She lived in the house across the street with her daughter, who had the biggest mouth of all the kids on the street. I could always tell when she was outside. She was a bossy little thing too, always telling the other kids what to do. She was a miniature version of her mother tall, athletic looking with long blondish hair. I was not sure how old the little girl was, and I was equally unsure about her mother's age.

She looked like she could be in her thirties; she was tall—I guessed her height to be around five feet eight inches. She had long blond hair, which she kept up most of the time, and a physique that must have been the result of a great deal of time in a gym. Her body was as toned and fit as I had ever seen.

It was her beauty and the way she moved that had me mesmerized. I had only seen her face clearly a few times when she walked on my front lawn to retrieve the toys her daughter had thrown. She was absolutely stunning, and she moved with the grace of a dancer; her muscles visibly flexing with every stride she took.

4

OK, I know I sound like a horny teenage boy, but somehow, I knew there was something very special about her and I was strangely drawn to her.

I would sometimes watch her daughter talking with her and see the little girl pointing toward my house when she spoke. I was not able to hear what they were saying, though I am sure they wondered about the mysterious man who lived here.

I had now spent the last ten months getting high every day, and I think I can safely say I had heard every song the Grateful Dead ever recorded. I had not read a newspaper, watched any television, or even looked at a computer screen since I moved into this house. I was not exactly thrilled by the fact that before I moved here, people were openly burning my photo or hanging me in effigy somewhere on a daily basis. It seemed to make the news constantly.

So, for the first time in my adult life, I had no idea about what was going on in the world. My little world at this point consisted of what was happening inside my house and as far as I could see out my front windows.

All that was about to change though. I had run out of pot, and my contact who had supplied it for me earlier would no longer take my calls.

Chapter Two

I did have cable and Internet service in my house. I decided it was time for me to turn on my television and see what I had been missing.

I expected that things would have gotten a bit worse, but I never thought it possible that the world would be in even more turmoil than before the time Zack first came to us.

It seemed like I had missed a lifetime of events. North Korea had a new leader. Uprisings were happening all over the Middle East, and in some cases, the leaders of these countries were killing their own people to remain in power. The Israelis were threatening to bomb Iran to keep them from obtaining a nuclear weapon…

It seemed there was some sort of conflict going on in every part of the world.

Here at home, we had our own share of problems. It was an election year, and the negativity had reached an all-time high. It made me wonder if this was what things were like in the 1860s before the Civil War.

We were anything but civil to each other. It seemed like rational discussion and compromise in our government had been replaced with name-calling and childish immaturity.

At first, I was amazed, even shocked, by what I saw, but those feelings soon turned to anger as I turned my attention to my laptop.

The Internet could be an amazing tool when used properly, but it could also be used to fuel hatred and prejudice.

When I saw images of our president being portrayed as an animal or as an infamous figure from history, it sickened me.

I started to become angry, and the more I saw, the angrier I became. The pot was gone, but I knew there was a box around here somewhere that had liquor in it. I needed a drink.

I had never been much of a drinker, and it was the middle of the day, but I found the box, opened a bottle of vodka, and started to drink it right from the bottle. I had the satellite radio blaring in the background, and Stevie Ray Vaughan's "Crossfire" began to play.

I started to sing along, doing my best air guitar with the now half-empty bottle of vodka.

Suddenly, I heard a commotion going on outside, and I turned the music off. The neighborhood kids were playing their version of stickball in the street in front of my house. I lived at the very end of the street, and since I never left, there were rarely cars driving by.

I decided to go outside to sit on my front porch and watch them play. I opened the front door and stepped out onto the porch. I turned to close the front door, and when I turned back to face the street, it hit me. I only felt it for a second; something slammed into my forehead and then nothing.

When I regained consciousness, the first thing I saw was the face of my neighbor from across the street. She was leaning over me, and I was lying on my couch. I could feel the cold on my forehead. I could also feel a throbbing pain in my right hand. I moved my hand to my face and realized that it was bandaged.

"You took one for the team," she said, holding up a hard rubber ball so I could see it.

"My hand?" I asked.

"You smashed it into one of the glass panes of your front door. No need to worry, though. Before I became a nurse practitioner, I was an operating room nurse for many years. You probably could have used some stitches, but I had a feeling you would not have wanted to go to the hospital, would you, Mr. Ryan?"

I started to sit up, and she put her hand on my chest to stop my movement. "You need to lie down; you took a pretty good hit to your head. Your secret is safe with me. Oh, and I called up one of my brothers. He will come replace the glass pane tomorrow."

"Thank you," was about all I could think to say at that moment. She started to walk toward the front door. "Please, wait," I said. "I'm very sorry. I guess I have been by myself for too long; I have forgotten my manners. What's your name?"

She chuckled and smiled. "My name is Missy Franzone, and my daughter, who thinks you're a fugitive from somewhere, is Kim."

"Thank you, Missy. I don't know how to repay you for this."

"Oh, I do," she said. "When you feel better, you and I have a lot to talk about. I'll be back in a few hours to check up on you, and I'll bring you some dinner. It looks like you've been living out of your microwave. You could use some real food."

Missy walked out my front door. I sat up from my couch to watch her. Her daughter was standing at the edge of her front lawn, and she ran over to hug her mother when she saw her coming toward her.

I quickly lay back down on the couch as both my head and my hand were killing me. It served me right for drinking in the middle of the day and on an empty stomach.

Well, if I wanted to meet the gorgeous neighbor from across the street, I probably couldn't have managed to do it in a worse way.

I started to run what had happened today through my head, sort of a "rewind of the day." What a shame we seemed to have learned nothing from Zack's presence among us. I started to doze off as I pondered the possibilities of what Missy wanted to talk about. What was the "a lot" she spoke of?

I felt a hand on my shoulder. "How are you feeling?" It was Missy leaning over me.

"I've been better." I groaned as I sat up. My head was still spinning.

"Here, drink this," I heard this little voice say to me in a bossy tone. A glass of orange juice was in Kim's hand, and she held it a few inches from my face.

"Thank you," I told her as I took the glass from her hand. It tasted great. I must have been very dehydrated because of all the vodka. I drank it down in one gulp and asked for more. After my second glass, I felt a bit more alive.

"You must be Kim," I said to the little girl standing in front of me. "My name is Michael."

"You look really bad," Kim replied as she studied my face. "My aunt Ann is coming to pick me up. Mom says you're a mess, and she needs to help you get your shit together."

"Kim!" Missy screamed from the kitchen. "Watch your mouth, young lady. You know you are not supposed to use those words."

"Well, I heard you talking to Aunt Ann, and that is what you told her," Kim replied in a defiant tone.

I laughed on the inside at the little girl's words. I had to admit her mother was right. My shit had not been together since that day in January 2010, when I was chosen to be the author of Zack's message.

I heard a horn beeping outside and looked through my front window. There was an SUV parked in my driveway. "That's my sister Ann," Missy said. "I'll be right back."

Kim walked up to me and put her hand on my head. "Mom says you're a good man; I hope you feel better soon. Bye, Michael," she said to me. Then she took her mother's hand and walked out the front door.

I watched as Missy put Kim in the backseat and then spoke with her sister. I could not hear what Missy said, but her sister had a loud voice and I was able to make out a few words, like *crazy*, *serial killer*, and *witness protection*. Missy stepped back from the SUV, waved to them, and began to walk back toward my house.

The front door opened; Missy came back in and walked over to my couch. "Come on; get up. You aren't crippled. You can make it to the table."

I got up off the couch. My head was still spinning a little bit, but I was upright. "I just need to use the bathroom, and I'll be right there."

I closed the bathroom door behind me, took what seemed like a five-minute piss, washed my hands, and looked at myself in the mirror as I cleaned my face. Kim was right; I did look really bad. I didn't recognize the face that was looking back at me. I shook my head in disgust, dried my hands, and left the bathroom.

I could smell the food as soon as I walked out of the bathroom, and it smelled damn good! I stood at the entrance of the dining room for a moment and watched as Missy set the table. Only yesterday, I was admiring this woman's beauty from a distance, and now she was in my house setting my table.

"Is there anything I can do to help?" I asked.

"No," Missy said. "Just sit down, and let's get some food in you." Missy began to bring the food to the table. It looked amazing! One platter was filled with veal and roasted peppers, another with spaghetti and red sauce. I was later told it was called "gravy," not sauce. The last dish was sautéed spinach, a favorite of mine.

Missy grabbed my plate and hefted on a pretty healthy portion of each dish. She placed the plate in front of me and then filled her own with much smaller portions than what she gave me. She sat down at the table, picked up her napkin, placed it on her lap, and looked over at me. I guess I must have been dazed; I just sat there and stared at her.

"Eat," Missy ordered.

I picked up my fork and dug in. It was amazing, like the food I had enjoyed in some of the finest Italian restaurants. "Wow, this is delicious. You should be a chef."

"Thank you," Missy said. "I enjoy cooking, and my mother taught all of us girls how to cook. She was old-fashioned—you know, the way to a man's heart is through his stomach."

"Well, your mother may have been old-fashioned, but she certainly taught you how to be a great cook."

Missy reached into the bag that was sitting on one of the dining room chairs. She pulled out a bottle of red wine and two glasses. She opened the bottle with expert precision and poured a little into each wineglass. She picked up one of the glasses and reached out to hand it to me.

"I'm not sure that having more alcohol would be a good thing for me right now," I said.

"Just have a little; it might help clear your head," Missy said as she handed me the glass.

I reached over and took the glass from her. I accidentally touched her hand as I did, and I swear I felt a tingle run through my body. I think she felt it too, judging by the expression on her face.

"Thank you. Thank you for the food, for the wine, and for coming to my rescue." I lifted my glass to toast. "To you, Missy Franzone!" We tapped glasses, and I had a sip of the wine. Like the food, the wine tasted great. Though I was no wine expert, I thought it was a perfect complement to the meal.

We finished our meal, and, as much as I enjoyed her company, the journalist in me began to come through. I started asking myself questions about Missy. The list began to grow: *Why is this beautiful woman sitting here with me? Why did she help me? Why would she keep my identity secret?* The big question I could not get out of my mind was: *what does she want from me?*

I decided to go fishing, so to speak, to see if I could get her to answer some of my questions. "You are so beautiful. Did you ever think of being a model?"

Missy smiled. "Before Kim was born, I was a fitness model for a short time. It was fun, but being judged solely for my looks got old pretty fast. I was always into a healthy lifestyle. I was a weight lifter, a personal trainer, and a yoga instructor when I was younger."

That explains the amazing body she has, I thought to myself. I decided to delve a bit deeper and see what else Missy would tell me about herself. "I noticed you do not wear a wedding band, Missy."

"Are you trying to interview me, Mr. Ryan?"

"No, of course not, and please call me Michael."

Missy got up from the table, walked over to her handbag, took out a copy of *Mr. Breeze*, and put it down on the table in front of me.

"It is my turn to ask the questions, Michael." I looked down at the book. I was still unsure of what she wanted. I had written everything that had happened when I was with Zack, and it was all recorded in that book.

"OK, I guess I owe you at least that much. Go ahead; ask away," I told her.

13

"Is he God?"

Well, at that moment, I learned one thing about Missy that I would always remember. She didn't beat around the bush. "Is he God?" she asked again, this time putting her index finger on the book. "Because, if he is, I need him to know what he let happen to me and to my daughter," she said, now pointing her finger at me. She was beginning to show her anger.

"I have asked myself that same question so many times," I told her. "This is what I have come to understand. He may be a god, but he isn't what we have always thought God was. There may be some being somewhere, even beyond what Zack is, but it is Zack we have always worshipped as our god. I don't know if that brings you any comfort, but it is at least what I have come to believe."

I saw her eyes begin to tear up, and she wiped them with her fingers. "I come from a very religious family, Michael. Like you, I was never really a believer, and I took some wrong turns when I was in my late teens and early twenties. Two of my brothers took me to a revival meeting. I was very moved by what I saw and felt that night, and it probably saved my life."

"I began to attend church every Sunday, and I tried to live a good life. I met and ended up falling in love with a remarkable man; his name was Steven Franzone. We were married and were very happy together. I had a very hard time getting pregnant, and we went to doctor after doctor for help. We even went as far as New York to see fertility specialists. I prayed to God every night for four damn years, Michael. I asked him to please give us a child."

"Finally, I got pregnant, and two months before Kim was born, Steven was killed in an accident. Do you know the woman who ran a red light and slammed into his car and killed him had three DUIs? She had just gotten her license back the day before the accident. I was told she was so drunk she didn't even know that she had been in an accident. Steven never even got to see his daughter. He was a good man, Michael. He did not deserve what happened to him; none of us did. The last time I entered a church was the day of Steven's funeral. I cursed God that day, Michael, and I no longer believe in anything."

"I am very sorry to hear that," I told Missy.

"You're sorry, Michael, I don't want or need your condolences. I want to believe again; I want to hear from Zack why he let Steven die."

Oh shit, I thought to myself, *she wants to speak with Zack. Does she somehow think I have a way to contact Zack?* "Missy, I hope you don't think I can just call out to Zack and he'll appear."

"You know, Michael, I watched what happened that day at the CDC. I recorded it, and I have watched it many times. I read *Mr. Breeze* so many times I think I now know it by heart. You were his messenger, Michael. What happened to you, how could you let yourself end up here looking this way?"

"The world thinks I'm dead, Missy, and except for a few close friends, and now you, I am dead. Since, like you said, you know Mr. Breeze by heart, you know I have no way to contact Zack and everything I did or thought was in one way or another his doing.

"I wrote a book, Missy; that is all I did, and I basked in the fame and the money it brought me. I was a fucking fool to believe that every religion on the planet was going to just heed his words and shut down. I doubt the Vatican wants to turn into a museum and bed-and-breakfast.

"You were a believer. I'm happy for you. Me? I never believed in anything, but after being with Zack, seeing his power, and feeling the aura around him, I began to believe in something more than myself. I knew he was giving me a great responsibility, but I wasn't exactly given a choice either, if you remember.

"So I did what he asked, and I went out there and told anyone who would listen, that man, not God, created religion and that his words and teachings had been used not to help mankind but to control it.

15

"As you can see by where I am now, that didn't go over as well as I expected. Did Zack send me help? No, Missy, he did not.

"Has he appeared even once since that day he left me with a bullet in my fucking leg? The answer is no, Missy; nor did he send me help when they started to call out for my life.

"Am I angry? You better believe I am. Do I blame Zack for what happened to me? No, Missy, I do not.

"I blame myself for believing that we had the ability to change. We do not. We are exactly what Zack thinks we are—nothing but disgusting animals."

I stood up from the table and began to pace around the room. I tended to do that when I was agitated or deep in thought. Missy took the copy of *Mr. Breeze* she had brought with her and held it up to my face.

"You know, Michael, the fucking bitch that killed my husband, do you know what happened to her? She hired a lawyer, and the lawyer convinced the judge she was sick and needed treatment, not jail. I wanted to wrap my hands around her neck and squeeze the life out of her myself, but I knew it would not bring Steven back, so I learned to live with my grief and loss. I also knew that I still had to have hope. If I can have hope, Michael, then you can too."

"Hope, Missy? Hope for what? That we all just kill each other and save Zack the trouble of doing it himself? I ran out of hope a while ago.

"Do you know why I got drunk? I had not turned on the television or my computer for almost a year, and when I did, I saw that things were even worse than they were when I first met Zack."

Missy began to speak. "I realize I may not be the heavenly father you have come to believe existed. That is my fault. I gave you that image when you were young. Though I did raise you and I chose to bestow free will upon you, you have used that gift to learn to hate, to kill, to become bitter and selfish, and to care only for yourselves. You have even learned to hurt your children and subjugate your fellow man. I tried to teach you the lessons you needed to learn to live in peace and harmony with each other, and you chose to ignore them. So, now, I give you one last chance to be what I always hoped you could be. Whether or not mankind continues is up to you. Learn well this time, my children; I will not be patient much longer."

Missy had just read the very words Zack had handed me that last day I saw him. The words he had told me to put at the end of the book. She knew them by heart. She hugged the copy of *Mr. Breeze* to her chest as she recited Zack's warning to me.

"Have you ever loved anyone, Michael, enough to die for them?"

"No, Missy, I have not."

"Well, if you had, you would understand why I would do anything to keep him from fulfilling his promise to destroy us."

"What do you think I can do, Missy? Last time I tried to save our sorry asses, it did not end all that well for me."

"Say something, Michael. Do something, anything, but don't hide in this house. Look at you! You were a handsome man. Have you looked in a mirror lately, Michael? You look like shit.

"The man who wrote this book was not a coward. He did not keep his mouth shut; he fucking stood up to God." I could tell Missy was getting really upset. She waved the copy of *Mr. Breeze* around as she spoke to me, her voice becoming louder.

"Maybe I am no longer that man, Missy. Maybe I came to realize we are like the dog that bites the hand that feeds it. You want me to let the world know I'm alive? Go out and spread the word. Please, the only fucking words anyone wants to hear these days are 'What's in it for me?'

"Fuck 'em, Missy. Fuck 'em all. You know, I really believe Zack knew that I would fail. He must have been laughing his ass off watching this whole thing." I could see by the look on Missy's face that my words did not please her.

"I am only one man, Missy, and one man cannot change the world."

"The man who wrote this book did not think that way," she said, holding the book out in front of her. "If that man ever comes back, my door is always open to him." She tossed the book onto the floor and stormed toward the front door. "I will keep your secret. After all, you're right; the real Michael Ryan is dead."

I watched Missy walk back to her house, and my first thought was what an asshole I was. Then I began to get angry. How dare this woman come in here and say those things to me. She wasn't there; she didn't see the hatred in the eyes of the people who wanted me dead.

She thinks she knows me, knows how I used to think. Well, fuck her too. I began to pace around the house, my mind swirling with questions. My anger had subsided, and I started to wonder whether Missy was right. Was I now a coward? Did I give up too easily? Was there something more I could have done? What should I do with all this food?

My thoughts turned to the kitchen and the dining room, and I walked in. There was food in containers, on the counter and on the plates at the table. Missy had left my house without taking back anything she had brought with her. I wasn't exactly great at cleaning, but I gave it my best shot. I put all the food away in the refrigerator, carefully washed off the plates, and put everything in the dishwasher, though I was not sure whether it actually worked or not. I hadn't used it once since I'd moved in here. I had chosen to use plastic utensils and cups, which I just rinsed off and used over again.

I found some dishwasher stuff under the sink, poured some in, and turned on the machine. It wasn't that late, but I was beat, so I decided to go to bed. Today was certainly not one of my better days. I was now beginning to feel like I had let people like Missy down and that Zack had made a big mistake. He picked the wrong man to carry his message.

I took three ibuprofen, drank a glass of water, and got into bed. *Shit, Michael you are a real fuck-up,* were my last thoughts as I drifted off to sleep.

Chapter Three

I awoke the next morning in a panic, my body covered in sweat. I had had the most vivid and frightening dream of my life, but it did not feel like a dream; it felt real.

I was standing with Zack and Rover, and he was making me watch as he destroyed our civilization bit by bit. I saw cities crumble and fall to the ground, billions and billions of people being killed. Then, near the end, Missy crawled up to Zack with Kim in her arms.

"Please spare her," Missy begged Zack. Then her eyes turned to me. "Michael, please do something, please, please, save her."

Zack looked at me. "You could have saved her, you could have saved them all Michael, but you did nothing." That was the last thing I remember.

It took me a couple of minutes to come to my senses as I just sat there in my bed. At first, I attributed the whole thing to a combination of vodka, rich food, and anger, but then I noticed my head and my hand were no longer in pain.

I lifted up my hand to my face. Missy had done a pretty good job of bandaging it up. Through the gauze, I touched the area that had been cut by the glass, and there was no pain at all!

I went into the kitchen and grabbed a pair of scissors to cut off the bandage. When I did, there was nothing—no blood, no cut, not even a mark.

I went over to look in the mirror and saw the bruise on my head was gone, as well.

"Zack, are you here?" I held my hand up over my head. "Zack, are you here?" I repeated. "Well, I guess you're not going to answer me. All right, I get the message. I'll do my best, but I need help. I cannot do this alone. And if you don't mind, please don't let them kill me."

I looked over at the clock on the oven. It was nine thirty in the morning. I went into the bathroom where I brushed my teeth, washed my face, and took care of business.

I threw on some clothes and walked out the front door. I had not been past my mailbox in all the time I lived here, but this time, I crossed the street and headed right for Missy's front door.

She answered the door wearing what looked to be her gym clothes. I held out my right hand to her. "Hi, my name is Michael Ryan, and I'm very glad to meet you."

Missy took my hand and smiled. "Missy Franzone. Very nice to finally meet you, Michael Ryan. I admire what you have done…Your head, what happened?" Missy then looked down at my hand and took hold of it. "You're healed. There isn't a mark on you. Even your scars are gone."

I stared at my hand. Missy was right; even the scars I had from old injuries were gone.

She grabbed my arm. "Come on; get in here," she ordered. "OK, so what happened, Michael?" Missy was staring at my forehead, moving her head from side to side. It was kind of annoying.

"What the fuck are you looking at?" I asked her, half smiling.

"Your forehead, there aren't any wrinkles!"

"Can I use your bathroom?" I asked. I was still in a bit of a fog and I still running everything that had happened in my dream or vision or whatever it was through my mind. In other words I was scared and confused.

Missy pointed to her right. "Sure; right over there." I walked into her bathroom and looked in the mirror. She was absolutely right; I had no wrinkles. I lifted my shirt and saw that all my scars were gone, even the one from the gunshot wound.

Come to think of it, my whole body felt different. At fifty-four, I had my share of aches and pains, but I felt none of that now. In fact, I realized I felt like I had when I was in my twenties. I left the bathroom and walked back to find Missy.

Her house was very different from mine. I don't know what style you would call it though. She had many photos in her house, and it looked like a home; it was warm and nicely decorated. One of the picture frames hanging on the wall held a copy of a fitness magazine cover. I walked over to take a closer look.

It was Missy wearing a two-piece workout outfit, though it looked more like a bikini. She was posed to show off her rather remarkable body; you could see her muscles flexed. She looked absolutely stunning.

"That was taken a long time ago, Michael," Missy said as she came up behind me. "Let's go sit down. You still have some explaining to do."

I followed Missy over to the couch and sat down. I told her about my dream, though considering what I had noticed since I'd woken up, I was certain it was not just a dream. I did not understand what it was.

"So you think Zack was sending you a message?" Missy asked.

"Missy, I don't think it was a message; it was a wake-up call, I think."

"What are you going to do about it, Michael?"

"Look, Missy, I'm sorry about what I said yesterday. You were right; I have been hiding. I have been hiding from myself. I may not be a hero, but I have never before been afraid of what anyone thought and I am too old to change now."

"So then, what are you going to do about it?" Missy asked me once again. I guess I had yet to give her the answer she was looking for.

"I may not be able to change the world, Missy, and maybe our fates have already been decided, but I am not going down without a fight. I know what Zack is now, and I know what he is capable of. I have no intention of sitting back on my ass and waiting for him to decide when our time is up."

"They will come after you again, Michael. You know that, right?"

"I know they will, Missy, but this time, I will not run and I will not back down. If those assholes are too fucking stupid to save their own lives, well then, I guess I am going to have to do it for them."

"So, what's our first move?" Missy stood up from the couch and started to pace back and forth. "Do you think we should issue a statement to the press stating that you are alive and living here? Or should we just show up at a news station?"

"Missy, what exactly do you mean with this 'we' stuff?"

"Well, I'm going with you, Michael," she announced.

"Oh no. No way, not a chance in hell that is happening, Missy. You said yourself they are going to come after me again. Well, I'm going to have enough to worry about just keeping myself safe. I'm not adding you and your daughter to that list."

"I asked you earlier, Michael, if you ever loved anyone enough to die for them. You told me you had not." I nodded my head in agreement with her words. "Well, I have. I do now, and I will do whatever I have to in order to save her. I am in this with you all the way, Michael Ryan. Like it or not, you are stuck with me."

I had to admit there were worse things in life than being stuck with the most beautiful woman you had ever seen, but I was still unsure Missy knew what she was getting herself into.

"And what about Kim? You said you would die for her, but you are putting her in danger by bringing her into this."

"I have no intention of bringing Kim along. My sister Ann lives a mile away, and Kim can stay with her. Look, Michael, you need me. And do not tell me you don't. You need someone to watch your back."

I do not know why, but for some reason, I knew I had to let her come with me, but I also knew it was crazy.

"All right, I think you're insane for wanting to do this, but I doubt I could stop you even if I tried."

"You got that right, bucko," Missy said, with a half-cocked smile on her face.

"Well, first thing I need is a haircut and a shave. I don't think this is the look I want to portray when I show the world I'm still alive."

"It just so happens that my sister Ann is pretty darn good with a pair of scissors. I'll go give her a call." Missy walked into her kitchen to phone her sister. Meanwhile, I still wasn't sure I was doing the right thing by letting her come with me. Hell, I wasn't even sure about what I was going to do.

"Ann will be over in about an hour. Come on in the kitchen; I'll make you some breakfast," Missy yelled out to me. I was kind of hungry, and I hadn't yet had any coffee this morning.

I walked into the kitchen; it was a woodworker's dream. The table and chairs were unlike anything I had ever seen before. They had exquisite carvings in them with Missy and Kim's names cut out in different design types. I didn't know enough about woodworking to be able to properly describe what I saw.

"Don't tell me you make furniture too?" I asked.

"No, this was all done by my dad."

"Your dad makes furniture for a living?"

"No, Michael, my dad owns a few restaurants; the woodworking is a hobby. You may have eaten at his restaurant in DC—Limberto's?"

"Wait, your family is Limberto's well, now the great food you cooked makes sense." Limberto's is considered the best Italian restaurant in the United States. "I have eaten there many times, Missy—always an amazing meal."

"Well, I'm glad to hear you liked it," Missy said, placing a cup of coffee on the table. She motioned for me to have a seat and then walked over to the stove.

I heard the sound of eggs cracking, and a few minutes later, a plate of scrambled eggs with spinach, mushrooms, and tomatoes was placed before me.

"Enjoy!" Missy said as she sat down across from me at the table. The eggs were out of this world. I had not had a breakfast like this in a long time.

"This is really good. Aren't you having anything?" I asked.

"No, I had a protein shake for breakfast after my workout," Missy replied.

I could never understand how anyone could drink that shit first thing in the morning, but I just smiled at her and nodded my head in agreement.

"So, Michael, is it true that you have never felt love?"

Oh shit. I had a feeling she would ask about that sooner or later. "Let's just say that up until I met Zack, I only believed in what I could see with my own eyes."

"And now?" Missy asked.

"Now, I'm open to everything. I no longer think anything is impossible. Zack was right about Julie, though. Julie was—"

"I know who Julie was, Michael. Remember, I read your book many times," Missy interrupted my sentence to announce.

"I have gone through a great many changes in the last two years, Missy, not all of them expected, but I still haven't ever felt love. I hope that it does happen to me someday."

"I'm sorry to hear that, Michael. Love is a unique feeling. I must admit though that it can be wonderful sometimes, but it can be incredibly painful as well." I wasn't sure how exactly to reply to her, and luckily, I didn't have to.

Missy's sister Ann came in the front door. "Hi, Miss, I'm here! Got my scissors and clippers. Where's the victim?"

"In here, Ann," Missy called out.

Ann walked back into the kitchen, and I stood up from my chair as she entered the room. "Whoa, somebody hasn't seen a barber in a long time," she said, giving me the once-over.

Ann looked a great deal like Missy, though she was a bit taller and her hair was darker and shorter. She certainly was fit, but she didn't have the ultra-toned body of her sister. Ann was obviously a little taken aback by seeing me at her sister's kitchen table.

"Ann, this is my neighbor, Michael."

I reached out my hand to Ann, and she stepped forward and reciprocated. "Very nice to meet you, Ann," I said.

"Same here," Ann replied, looking over at her sister.

"OK, where are we going to do this, Miss, the downstairs bathroom?"

"That's as good a place as any," Missy replied.

"Come on," Ann said motioning for me to follow her. I gulped down my last bit of coffee and followed Ann into the bathroom.

Missy walked in after us, carrying a chair in one hand and a stack of newspapers in the other. She placed the chair in front of the mirror and grabbed my shoulders. She gently prodded me to sit down in the chair. She took the newspapers and unfolded them, placing them all around the floor beneath and around the chair. I half wanted to reach down and grab one of them. I hadn't read one in a long time.

"OK, he's ready for you," Missy said looking over at her sister.

Ann plugged in the clippers and started to run her hands through my hair. "You have nice hair, just way too damn much of it!" she told me.

I thanked her, but since I was pretty certain Missy hadn't told her sister who I was, I was doing my best not to engage in any conversation that would require me to tell her about myself.

Ann started to cut my hair, and I saw big clumps of it hitting the newspapers that covered the floor. "How short do you want me to go?"

"Pretty short, but not above the ears," I replied.

Ann continued to cut, switching between the clippers, scissors, and a comb as needed.

"I never heard my sister mention you before, and now here you are. What gives?"

I wasn't sure what to say, but she was almost done, and I wasn't about to upset someone with scissors in her hands. "Your sister just showed me some kindness," I said.

I saw Ann's reflection in the mirror. She was not buying that response.

"Well, there you go. You're going to have to shave all that hair off your face yourself. That, I do not touch!"

"Thank you, Ann, I really appreciate this."

Missy came walking into the bathroom with a razor in her hand.

"You're going to need this, and these too," Missy told me as she placed the razor, extra blades, a grooming thingy, and shaving cream on the sink.

"Thanks. This might take a while," I replied. Missy and Ann left me alone in the bathroom. It was hard for me to see for sure under my year-long beard, but my face did seem different.

I was fairly confident Ann was out there interrogating Missy about me and what I was doing in her house. I had no idea how Ann was going to react once I was clean-shaven and she realized who I was. I had become a polarizing figure, and I didn't know if she felt the same way as her sister or if she was one of those who had cheered my demise.

I had never gone more than a week without shaving before, and getting a year's worth of growth off was not as easy as it sounded. It took me about twenty-five minutes with the scissors, the trimmer, and the razor to get myself clean-shaven again.

I washed my face to get all the excess shaving cream off and looked at myself in the mirror. Wow, I was a little shocked by my reflection! I looked like I did twenty years ago, not like I did the last time I saw myself without long hair and a beard. I guessed Zack had done more than just heal some wounds and remove my scars.

I suddenly felt empowered again, like I used to when I was chasing stories. I was a fearless fuck back then; I never backed down from anything or anyone. *Well, here goes nothing,* I thought, as I left the bathroom.

Missy and Ann were sitting at the kitchen table when I walked in. "Well, it's good to be back among the living," I said to them both. That was probably not the best choice of words considering the situation. Missy looked at me and smiled. I think she liked what she saw, though her sister Ann had quite a different reaction.

Ann stood up from her chair at the table. "You're dead! I saw it! You burned to death." Then, once the shock of seeing me alive passed, she looked over at Missy. "Are you fucking crazy?" she screamed at her sister. "What the hell are you doing with Michael Ryan in your house? Do you know what those religious freaks would do to you and to Kim if they found out you had him here?"

Missy stood up from the table and walked over to me. She ran her right palm across my face.

"Could you give Ann and me some time to talk in private?" she asked me.

"Sure. I'll be across the street, and if you change your mind, I will certainly understand."

"No one is changing my mind, Michael. I will see you soon, and I really like the new look."

I said my good-byes to Ann, who was definitely not sorry to see me leave, and then I walked back across the street to my house.

30

There was one thing I had chosen not to tell Missy about my dream or whatever it was. It was that I knew that our time was almost up. Zack wouldn't wait much longer before he acted. Maybe I should not have kept this from her, but I thought it best, at least for the time being.

I also didn't tell her I really didn't have a plan. In fact, I hadn't even thought past the first step.

I started to look around the house, and I realized there was nothing there that I really cared about. Everything that had ever mattered to me had been destroyed in the fire. All I had left to take with me was a laptop and my suitcase of clothes.

I still wasn't sure what Missy was going to do. I was certain her sister was over there doing her best to talk her out of coming with me. I figured if that failed, she just wouldn't agree to look after Kim, and I knew that would stop Missy.

It was only about fifteen minutes before Missy was at my front door. She knocked and walked in. "Can you wait until Kim gets out of school before we get started?" she asked.

"Sure. I didn't know if you would still be coming," I answered.

Missy smiled. "I think you need to learn your first lesson about me right now, Michael. I am stubborn and hardheaded. I don't give up once I start something, and I give whatever I'm doing my all."

"All right then, I will remember that," I told her. I had a feeling Missy might be a bit more complex than I first thought. I was looking forward to finding that out. "The first thing we are going to need is money—a lot of it."

Missy nodded her head in agreement and said, "And we get that where?"

"Well, Missy, selling a few hundred million copies of a book does earn one some pretty hefty royalties." I could see by the look on her face she didn't realize how wealthy I was. "Yes, Missy, I made money on every book that was sold."

"How much did you make on each book?"

"Well, the formula is a bit complicated, but let's say an average of seven dollars."

Missy's expression turned to one of shock. "You must have made a billion dollars. Holy shit, you're a fucking billionaire!" She started to chuckle.

"Is something funny?" I asked.

"Nope," she replied.

I did need to get to the money, and in order to do that, I was going to need one of the few people who knew I was still alive, my attorney, Marty Charles.

Marty and I came up with a code name I should use if I ever needed to call him. It was for my safety. If I had to call one of his offices and leave a message, I could not exactly say, "Have him call Michael Ryan."

I grabbed my cell phone and called Hartman, Silverman, Charles, and Cohen. When the receptionist answered, I asked for Marty. When she asked who was calling, I answered, "Mr. Cruise." Marty had thought of that code name since he and his wife loved to take cruises.

"Well, it is good to hear from you, Michael. How are you doing?" Marty had one of those upbeat voices, he always sounded like he was about to start to try and sell you something.

"I'm fine, Marty, in fact, better than fine, and I need to see you."

"Really! Michael, are you sure that's a good idea?"

"Yes, Marty, it is. I'm done hiding, and I need to see you today. Which office are you working in?"

"I am down in DC today, Michael, and if you insist on coming, I can see you here."

"Thanks, Marty. I don't think I can make it till around seven; will that work for you?"

"Sure, Michael, I'll still be here. Can you at least give me a clue as to what is so important?"

"I'll see you around seven; we'll discuss it then."

"All right, see you later, Michael."

Marty hung up. I am sure he was trying to figure out what was so important that I needed to see him today and without prior notice.

"You didn't tell him very much. Why?" Missy asked me.

"I made a lot of mistakes during the last two years, and one big one I made can be fixed. That is the first thing I need you to help me with."

"What are we talking about, Michael?"

"I made a shitload of money from all the copies of Mr. Breeze that sold, as well as appearances and speaking engagements, and you know what I did with all that money? I did nothing with it, Missy. I bought a nice house, some nice things, but I didn't use it for a single worthwhile cause. I'm about to change that. I want you to find some good charities for that money. Give to those whom you feel need it. Spread it around, and let it do some good for people. Will you do that for me?"

Missy smiled. "I would be more than happy to help with that. You are starting to surprise me, Michael Ryan. You might not be as big an asshole as I thought."

"Well, thanks, Missy."

"Can I ask you something, Michael?"

"Sure, Missy, you can ask me anything you want."

"OK, what was it like to never believe in anything and to never have faith?"

I thought for a moment before I answered her. I had learned that voicing my views on religion tended to rub some people the wrong way, but Missy deserved a straight answer.

"For me, Missy, belief and faith are two very different things. I have faith in myself, but I never believed in things just because I was told I was supposed to. After I met Zack and learned what I did, I realized that I was justified in my non belief."

"So, you still don't believe?" Missy asked.

"On no, Missy, on the contrary. I believe in what I saw. I believe Zack is the god we have believed in and worshipped for thousands of years. I honestly believe he will do exactly what he said he would if we do not show him we are capable of change. These things, I believe in."

"Well, Michael, I need to go get some things in order. Kim will be home from school today at twelve thirty, and if it is OK with you, I'd like to spend a little time with her before we leave."

"Of course, Missy. I understand. I'll be at your house at two o'clock."

"By the way, Michael, how exactly are we going to get to DC? I peeked in your garage, and you don't have a car." I had forgotten I didn't have a car. Cars required registration and insurance, and those things meant having my name out there. And that was one thing I definitely didn't want when I came here.

Missy chuckled. "Don't worry, Michael. I have no problem driving. I'll see you in a few hours." Missy walked out the front door and headed back across the street. *No car,* I thought to myself. What a moron I was. I hadn't even thought far enough ahead to figure out transportation.

I spent the next few hours getting the house straightened up. I knew no matter what happened I would probably never come back here again. I packed the few clothes I had into my travel bag, grabbed my laptop, went out to my front porch, and sat down.

I still didn't truly understand why Zack picked me out of all the people on this planet. Why the fuck was I the one he chose? I was nothing special; I had never done anything spectacular or anything that would benefit my fellow man. Hell, I was a loner and didn't even like my fellow man all that much.

I found most of them annoying, superficial assholes. I had never been a loving person; in fact, I was generally distant and cold. I had never even truly been in love, and I had never trusted anyone. I remembered Zack had told me he chose me because I never believed in anything and I could write, but somehow, that was never enough of a reason for me.

I knew what I had to do. I just wished I knew what Zack saw in me that I never did.

35

Chapter Four

I watched the school bus come down the street. First, it was flashing yellow lights, and then the lights turned red and the safety bar swung out to its side as it came to a stop. The children got off the bus laughing and yelling things I couldn't completely make out as they ran toward their houses.

I watched the bus stop in front of Missy's house. Missy came out the front door of her house as the bus doors opened. Kim got off and ran to her mother. She gave her a hug when she reached her. I had never had children, and I had given up on ever having them a long time ago. It was something I would always regret.

Missy walked Kim into the house, and about twenty minutes later, I saw a car pull up in front of her house. It was her sister Ann and a man. I assumed he was Ann's husband or boyfriend. They both looked over in my direction but didn't bother to wave. It was another half hour before I saw Missy's garage door open and heard the sound of a car starting.

The engine rumbled as it ran. I saw the reverse lights come on as it pulled out of the garage. It had the round BMW symbol on the back along with the model designation M3. The car was white, and it had four shiny exhaust pipes protruding out the back and a little black piece on the top of the trunk, which I thought they called a spoiler. The car had a sound of great power as it idled.

Missy got out of the car, looked at me, and motioned for me to come over. I walked across the street and stopped at the passenger door. "Nice car," I said. I still did not know that much about cars but had learned that when people bought nice cars or watches or anything, they wanted you to notice, so it was polite to acknowledge them.

"Do you know about cars, Michael?" Missy asked.

"I know how to drive. That is about it. I never had time for the car hobby," I answered.

"This is an M3, though it has had a few modifications," Missy told me. I could tell she was proud of her car, and I didn't want to let on that I really couldn't care less about what kind of car she drove.

Kim came running out of the house and stopped right in front of me. "Mom says you're going to help people, and she's going with you to help. Why do you need my mom's help?" Kim asked me. I had no idea how to talk to a little girl, nor did I have a clue as to what Missy had told her.

"Well," I said. Then, Missy chimed in, cutting me off. "I told you, honey, Michael needs me to help him with paperwork and to give food and clothes to kids like you who do not have enough."

"OK," Kim said seeming satisfied with her mother's explanation. "My mom says you're a good man, so is it OK if I give you a hug good-bye?"

"Yes, it is," I said, and I crouched down until we were the same height.

Kim put her arms around my neck and hugged me. I reciprocated. Kim whispered in my ear, "Mom says you're very handsome."

I smiled, and Kim let go and backed away. I stood up and saw Ann and the man she came with walking toward me. "Tom," Ann ordered, "leave it be."

"Michael, this is my brother Tom," Missy said.

I put my hand out to shake Tom's hand, but he brushed it aside and grabbed the front of my shirt.

"I know who you are and what you are, and if anything happens to my sister, I am going to fucking rip out your heart." Tom was a big, strong guy, and I had no doubt he could do exactly what he just threatened.

"Mom, look at that big dog!" Kim yelled out.

"Tom, get away from him," Ann said in a commanding voice. "Tom, do it now," she said, this time grabbing his shoulder, trying to pull him away from me.

I heard a growl, and I looked across the street. It was Rover the sable and black German Sheppard Zack had transformed during our time together. He was sitting on the front lawn of my house, about two feet from the street. Even sitting down, he must have been seven feet tall. Rover stood up and started to walk toward us. Tom quickly let go of me and began to back up with his hands in the air.

"Michael, please!" Missy screamed.

Rover started walking, and once he reached the middle of the street, he lifted one of his front paws and slammed it down onto the street. The ground shook beneath us, and the sidewalks up and down the street started to crack.

He began walking toward us again, and this time, he stopped at the edge of Missy's lawn, a few steps from the street. He was watching Tom, his sharp teeth showing, his snout curled.

The last time I'd seen Rover, he had saved my life, but that was two years ago and I wasn't sure if he would even listen to me now. I decided to give it a try. I started to walk slowly toward him, and he turned from looking at Tom to me. "Hi, Rover. It's good to see you, boy! Everything is OK; no one is going to hurt me, OK." I motioned back toward where Tom and Ann were standing. They both nodded their heads in agreement.

Rover looked over at them and then glanced at Missy and Kim. He turned around and started to walk back across the street, vanishing before he reached my front lawn. I turned around and walked back toward Ann and Tom. I walked up to Tom and once again held my hand out to him.

This time, he shook my hand. "I will promise you this. I will do whatever is within my power to protect your sister," I said. Tom said nothing in reply as we finished shaking hands and I walked back toward the car. I opened the side door, pulled the seat forward, and put my bag and my laptop in the backseat. I got in the passenger seat, closed the door, and waited for Missy.

I was surprised by how comfortable the seats were; they seemed to grab you on the sides. I was also surprised to see that the car had a manual transmission. The top of the gearshift lever had a large M on it. On the driver's side, I saw a pair of loafers on the floor mat, but I wasn't sure what they were for. I soon found out when Missy opened the driver's door and got in. Sitting sideways with her back to me, she reached down with her right hand and grabbed the loafers. Then she slipped off her high-heeled shoes and put the loafers on.

I realized they were driving shoes. It would have been very hard to drive a manual car with four-inch heels. Missy pulled out of her driveway, and she waved to everyone as we drove away. As we headed on our way, I took one last look at the house that I had called home.

"So, what was that all about? Why do you think Rover suddenly appeared?" Missy asked me.

I had to admit I was wondering the same thing. Tom wasn't trying to hurt me, certainly not like the people who tried to broil me in my own house. Zack or Rover never appeared to me back then, why now? "I honestly have no fucking clue," I answered.

"So, how well do you know this Marty guy, Michael? Do you trust him?" I heard Missy, but I was deep in thought. I was replaying in my mind what had happened just before we left. Rover had to have known that Missy's brother wasn't actually going to harm me. He was only being protective of his sister. So why did he appear? Was this another message from Zack, and, if it was, what the fuck was he trying to tell me?

"Michael, are you listening to me?" Missy asked.

"Sorry, I was just running some stuff through my head. I've known Marty a long time, Missy. His firm was big-time into lobbying, and I met him when I was doing a story on corruption in DC. Marty was clean, and we became friends. He was the one who introduced me to Julie."

"Oh, the one who left you after *Mr. Breeze* came out," Missy said.

"Yes, that one," I replied.

Missy drove like a maniac, weaving in and out of traffic. She always had two hands on the wheel unless she was shifting gears, which she did with lightning speed. She drove like she was on a racetrack, not a highway. She noticed I was watching her. "My husband was a stock-car racer, Michael; he taught me about cars. How to drive them and how to make them better. If you don't mind, I need to stop somewhere before we meet your attorney," Missy said.

"Where do you need to go?" I asked.

"Limberto's. I want to see my parents. My sister Joan called them and told them everything, Michael. They are preparing quite a feast for us. Are you OK with us stopping there?"

"Hey, we have to eat, and it might as well be in one of the best restaurants in the country. Sure, that works for me. Though, if you don't mind, I'd like to get there in one piece. Please slow down just a little."

Missy smiled and pushed her foot down harder on the accelerator.

I learned something else about Missy right then. She didn't like being told what to do. We made it to Georgetown in a little over two hours and pulled up to Limberto's at about five o'clock. The valet was waiting for us by the front door. Missy pulled up the hand brake, shook the shifter to make sure it was in neutral, and put her hand on the door handle. I put my left hand on her right wrist, and she looked over at me.

"Am I a saint or a sinner in there?" I asked her.

"Michael, my parents are good people. They are old school, but my mother was diagnosed with cancer three years ago and then Zack came. And now, no more cancer! You are no sinner here, Michael. Come on; let's eat."

The valet had come around to open Missy's car door, and as she stepped out, she gave the man a hug. "How have you been, Eduardo?" she asked him.

"I am good, Miss Limberto! Where is the little one?" the Latin man asked.

"She is home with my sister, Ann. This is my friend, Michael."

Eduardo reached his hand out to me. "Nice to meet you, Señor Michael."

I shook hands with Eduardo. "It's nice to meet you, as well, Eduardo," I replied.

We walked into the restaurant, and Missy's sister, a tall woman with long dark hair, was the first one to greet us. "Hi, Sis," she said as she and Missy hugged.

"Michael, this is my sister Joan. She is the business side of the Limberto brand." Joan stepped over to me, and I reached out my hand, but she gave me a hug instead. "I have always wanted to meet you, Michael, to thank you for everything you did."

"We all want to thank you," came a man's voice.

I turned my head and saw Angelo Limberto standing a few feet away. These days, chefs like Angelo were as famous as movie stars, and their faces were easy to recognize. I was glad to get such a warm welcome.

Missy went over and gave her father a big hug and a kiss. "Hi, Pop," she said.

"Missy, come here, my little baby," Missy's mother said as she came toward us.

Missy hugged and kissed her mother. It was very nice to see a family so close and so loving. I was not fortunate enough to come from such a family. In fact, I always thought my parents had had a child because that was what the manual told them to do. I didn't think they were ever very good at being parents, and they never seemed to want to be. I went off to college at seventeen, and we had only spoken maybe a half dozen times before they died in a boating accident when I was twenty-three.

"Mom, Dad, I'd like you to meet my friend—"

"I know who this is," Missy's mom interrupted. She walked over to me, put her hands on both sides of my cheeks, and then gave me a hug. "Thank you for fighting for us all, Michael Ryan," she said to me.

"Thank you, Mrs. Limberto," I said.

"You can call me Franny, Michael; all my friends do," Missy's mom replied.

Franny turned her attention back to her daughter and asked Missy how Kim was and whether she had brought any new pictures with her. Joan was still standing next to me.

"You have a very wonderful family," I said to her.

"Yes, thank you, Michael, I do. Can I talk to you alone for a few minutes?" Joan asked.

43

"Sure," I said.

Joan motioned for me to follow her, and we sat down at a table far enough away so that Missy's parents could not hear us.

"He is coming back, isn't he, Michael?" Joan asked me.

"Yes, Joan, he is. I do not know when, but I think it will be sooner rather than later," I replied.

Joan said, "I want to apologize for Ann's and Tom's behavior toward you. They are just like the rest of our family—protective. We bear you no ill will; they were just doing their best to look out for Missy. You know, Michael, Missy is a lot more than just a pretty face. My sister is a very smart girl, and she doesn't trust easily, but she trusts you, so I trust you."

"Thank you, Joan. What made you think Zack was coming back?" I asked.

"Missy told me about your dream, and she was the one who told me Zack was coming. Michael, she is with you because she wants to help you save all of us. That is what you are doing here, right?" Joan asked.

It seemed I might not have given Missy enough credit. She was a lot more than just a gorgeous face and an amazing body.

"Yes, Joan, that is what we are trying to do. I don't know whether it is too late for us or not, but if it is, I want it to end with me fighting for every last one of us," I told her.

"If there is anything any of us can do to help you, please just ask."

"Thanks, Joan."

"I think they are ready to start dinner," Joan announced as she got up from the chair.

I followed her over to the round table where Missy, Franny, and Angelo were sitting. "Sit here, Michael, next to me," Missy said, tapping the empty chair beside her.

Missy smiled at me as I sat down. I was beginning to realize that it was going to be very difficult to be around her and not feel something. Missy was everything any man could ever want. It had been a long time since I had felt anything for anyone, but I was beginning to have feelings for her. I was unsure what, if anything, she felt for me or even if the feelings I was beginning to have for her were the smart way to go.

"So, looking around this table, I guess I am going to have to be the one to say grace," Franny said. Missy and I just looked at each other and sat there while Franny recited a prayer. Joan and Angelo joined her. When she was done, the food began to come out of the kitchen. The waiters first brought antipasto, which was delicious.

Limberto's was famous for making everything in-house. They cured their meats and even made their own cheeses. After the antipasto came platters of various pastas, veal scaloppine, and a large plate of whole grilled fish. Angelo stood up and expertly fileted them for everyone. It was the best meal I had ever had! At one point, I saw Franny whisper something to one of the waitresses, and she returned with a magazine, which she handed Franny. Franny opened it up and started looking through the pages.

"So, Michael, I have to say, whoever did your work did a great job!" Franny exclaimed.

"Mom, geez, leave him alone with that stuff!"

"What I would just like to know is, who did it? You know I'm not getting any younger," Franny told Missy.

"Work? What do you mean work?" I asked.

45

"Your face, Michael. This is my mom's way of asking how you look so young," Missy said. I finally understood. Franny thought I'd had plastic surgery. I bet the magazine she had in her hand had a picture of me in it.

I smiled at Franny. "Franny, Zack made me this way, and I have a feeling he is not taking on any new patients," I said. My reply gave everyone at the table a chuckle.

By the time we finished our meal, it was almost six thirty. I showed Missy the time on my watch, and she nodded her head in acknowledgement. "Mom, Dad, Joan, I am sorry, but Michael and I must be going. We have an appointment at seven." I watched as Missy hugged her parents and her sister, and then I walked over to say my good-byes.

"Thank you all for making me feel so welcome and for the most amazing meal I've ever had." I shook Angelo's hand, and Franny came over, gave me a big hug, and kissed my cheek.

"You watch out for my little girl," she told me.

"I promise I will," I replied.

Joan walked out to the street with us. Eduardo was waiting out there, and Missy's car had already been brought around front.

"You remember what I said, Michael," Joan said to me as she gave me a hug.

"I will, Joan. Thank you, again," I told her, and then I got in the passenger side of the car. We drove down to K Street and sent Marty a text message that we were a few minutes away.

Missy laughed when she saw my rather archaic phone. "Why don't you get yourself a real phone?" she teased me, holding up her shiny touch-screen smart phone.

"This one works just fine for me," I told her. I was never really a gadget guy and could never understand people's obsession with them. I used to see people walking down the street with their eyes locked on their phone screens. I wondered if they realized that they looked like programmed robots from a science fiction movie. I thought that was part of what Zack meant when he said our technology was making us less human.

Instead of becoming more informed, we tuned out what we didn't want to know and used these devices to hide from reality—or at least the realities we were not interested in dealing with.

We pulled into the underground garage beneath Marty's building. Hartman, Silverman, Charles, and Cohen occupied the top four floors of the building, and Marty's office was on the top floor. After the last two lobbying scandals, Marty had secured his position as the "go-to" guy in DC. However, Marty would never refer to himself as a lobbyist. He would call himself a *facilitator*. The truth was that Marty was 25 percent lawyer, 25 percent lobbyist, and 50 percent schmoozer.

He had a way of getting you to agree with him and think it was your own idea. We found a parking spot right near the elevators. I was surprised how many cars were still there this late in the day. We got in the elevator, and I pushed button eleven. The Buildings Act prevented buildings in DC from being too tall, and, if my memory served me, there was only one office building over two hundred feet in the whole city.

Marty was standing there waiting for us when the elevator doors opened. He was a year younger than I and about the same height. He had kept himself in good shape over the years and was always dressed in the finest suits. He used to laugh at me saying I looked like I slept in my clothes. Marty's eyes opened as wide as they could go when he saw me. "What the hell happened to you?" were the first words out of his mouth.

"Nice to see you too, Marty," I said, reaching out my hand to shake his. Marty just kept staring at me. "Marty, I'd like you to meet Missy Franzone."

Marty turned his head for a moment toward Missy. "Nice to meet you," he said and turned his gaze right back to me.

"Michael, you look like you are thirty. What happened to you? This is not computing for me," he said, looking me up and down. "I've seen the best work money can buy, and that could not even come close to what I'm seeing here," he said.

"Can we please go to your office? I will explain everything to you," I said.

Marty looked over at Missy again, realizing he had slighted her earlier, and reached his hand out to her. "I am so sorry, but I was a little shocked at Michael's appearance. I'm Marty Charles, and it's very nice to meet you, Missy."

"It's a pleasure to meet you too, Marty," Missy said as they shook hands. Marty led us back to his office. His space was fairly large, and Missy and I sat in two very comfortable leather chairs facing Marty's desk. I told Marty about my dream and how I had woken up like this, looking like I did when I was thirty. I also told him about Rover's appearance at Missy's house. Marty listened intently, not interrupting me once while I spoke.

"So, what do you think all this means?" Marty asked when I was finished.

"I am not a hundred percent sure, but my gut tells me I need to do something to make people understand Zack's message and that his patience with us is running out," I said.

"You already did what he asked you to do Michael. You wrote the book," Marty replied.

"Yeah, Marty, I wrote the book and I got rich, but what did I do besides bask in my fame? I'll tell you what I did. Nothing, not one single decent thing. Well, that all changes today, and that is why I am here," I told him.

"So, what can I do to help you?" Marty inquired.

"First off, how much money do I have?" I asked.

"Do you mean liquid assets or investments like real estate?" Marty replied.

"For now, liquid," I told him.

Marty turned to his computer screen and started writing things down on the pad in front of him. This process took a few minutes. When he was done, he gave me one of those "Can I talk in front of her?" looks.

"It's OK, Marty; you can talk in front of Missy," I reassured him.

"This is not an exact number, Michael. When you're talking numbers like these, it is hard to be exact with just a quick check," Marty said.

"So, how much?" I asked.

"One point two billion, give or take," Marty said.

Missy gasped. I looked over at her. "I told you I sold a lot of books! All right, Marty, this is what I want you to do. I want you to put ten million in an account with my name. Get me two credit cards linked to that account: one in my name, the other in the name of Missy Franzone.

"Then I need to open two other accounts. One in the name of Missy Franzone and the other in the name of Kim Franzone. Kim's will need to have Missy's sister, Ann, as trustee. Missy will give your people the details. I want each one of those accounts to be for fifty million dollars."

Marty put down his pen and looked over at me. "Michael, can we speak in private please?" he asked.

Missy grabbed my arm at the same time Marty put down his pen. "What are you doing, Michael? I never asked you for anything like this," she said to me.

"I'll explain in a minute. Let me go talk to Marty," I told her.

Missy nodded in agreement, and I followed Marty into the conference room down the hall.

Once we were inside, Marty closed the door. "Have you lost your fucking mind?" he asked me. "That might be the most beautiful woman I have ever seen, but fifty million dollars! Michael, why?" Marty asked.

I knew Marty, and I realized he was only trying to protect me, both as my attorney and as my friend. "First of all, she and I are not involved. In fact, I have never even kissed her. For some unknown reason, she is risking her life to help me, and if this all blows up in our faces, she is going to need money, Marty. Money to hide, money to live somewhere that she and her daughter can be safe. And if for some reason, we both don't make it, her daughter will be well taken care of. Money is the only thing I have to give to say thank you for what she is doing. Can you understand that?" I asked him.

"All right, buddy, I will do whatever you want. You really haven't even kissed her?" Marty smiled. "You might want to work on trying to change that." We walked back into his office.

Missy was still sitting in her chair. Once I sat back down, she turned to look at me. "Please explain this to me," she asked.

I explained everything as I had told it to Marty and gave her my reasoning for what I did. She seemed to accept it, though begrudgingly. "OK, I will go along with this as long as you understand that my reasons for being here have nothing to do with money," Missy said.

"So, what else are you planning to do, Michael?" Marty asked.

"I want you to take the rest of the money and make it available for distribution," I told him.

"Distribution? Distribution where, Michael?" Marty asked, sounding puzzled.

"We're going to give it all away, Marty—every last dime of it—and Missy is going to be responsible for making sure it gets to those who need it," I told them both.

I looked over at Missy. She seemed a bit stunned, and Marty looked pretty much the same. They stayed like that for about thirty seconds, and then Missy turned her head and looked over at me. She nodded her head and gave me a big smile.

"Michael, we are not set up here to function as a charity. I'm not sure how much help we can be with the distribution of your money," Marty said. "I do have partners, but they are not in the 'giving money away' business."

"Of course, Marty, I can understand that you're a businessman and you need to make money. So bill me twenty-five million dollars and get Missy whatever she needs in order to accomplish what I asked."

Marty smiled. "I am sure we can help Ms. Franzone accomplish this goal. I will get started on this right away. Anything else?" Marty asked.

"Oh, one more thing. You must have a condo or two that you let your special clients use when they are in town, right?" I asked Marty. He nodded in acknowledgment. "Are any of them empty?" I asked.

Marty looked at his computer screen. "Yes, Michael, as a matter of fact, the three-bedroom unit over in Chevy Chase is not being used right now."

"Good. We are going to need a place to stay until your people set up the accounts and get us those credit cards."

"I'll go get you the keys," Marty said, getting up from his desk. He walked out of the office leaving Missy and me alone.

"Are you sure you're OK with this? You know you can still go back home; no one knows about you yet," I told her.

"Michael, for the last time, please stop asking me if I want to leave. I told you I am in this till the end, and I meant it. You are actually starting to piss me off."

I decided that would be the last time I would ask Missy that question. She did not need, or want, my protection, and I needed to be respectful of her wishes.

Marty came back into the office with an envelope, which he handed to me. "Everything you need is in there: keys, garage pass, alarm code, and a list of restaurants that deliver food. Those restaurants will charge it to our account. Michael, it might take a day or two to get all of this together, so stay there as long as you need to," he told me.

"Thanks, Marty," I replied.

Marty handed Missy a piece of paper."Ms. Franzone, here is my assistant's name and number. Call her tomorrow morning. She will need to get some information from you, and once she is done with the paperwork, she'll bring it over to you for your signature."

"Nancy will need to bring you papers to sign, as well, Michael, but we have all your information here."

"OK, Marty, whatever you need to get this done," I told him.

Missy and I said our good-byes, and Marty walked us back to the elevator. He held the door open as Missy walked in first. "Hey, buddy," he said to me as I entered the elevator. I looked over at him, and he gave me the thumbs-up. I smiled as the elevator doors closed.

We got back into Missy's car, and I opened the envelope Marty had given me. "So where are we going?" Missy asked.

"North Park Avenue, off Wisconsin. Do you know where that is?" I asked.

"I went to school down here, Michael. I know this town very well."

We made it to the condo in about fifteen minutes, as there was almost no traffic. This time, Missy drove like a sane person, not an Indy driver. I gave her the garage pass, and the gates opened up. "We need to park in the spots for 11E," I told her. We found the parking spaces allotted for the condo, parked, and unloaded our stuff from the car.

All I had was my shoulder bag and my laptop. Missy had a wheeled suitcase and a smaller tote bag. "What?" she asked me. She had seen me staring at her as she grabbed the handle of the suitcase.

"Nothing," I replied.

She smiled and handed me the smaller bag. "Make some use of yourself," she told me.

We found our way to the elevator and up to the eleventh floor. The number on the key was 1108; it was located at the end of the hall. I opened the door and heard the beeping sound of the alarm system. I punched in the code Marty had given me. The system disarmed. Missy found the light switches and flipped them on. "Nice place, but it is stuffy in here," she said. I found the temperature control unit and lowered it down to seventy degrees. I could hear the system turn on.

I looked around the place. It was very nicely furnished, and, of course, it had a fully stocked bar and a wine refrigerator. I walked through the rest of the condo checking out each bedroom. The largest one had a Jacuzzi and steam shower in it. When I was done, I found Missy in the kitchen with a bottle of water in her hand. "We'll be fine if we can survive on beer and water," she said, opening up the refrigerator door to show me.

"Well, there are some menus in that envelope. Marty said they would deliver food to us. I think we are going to be here a few days," I told her.

"OK, which bedroom is mine?" she asked. I pointed to the door of the largest bedroom, and she walked over and took a peek inside. Then she looked at the other two bedrooms as she returned to the kitchen. "Thank you, Michael, but you do not need to give me the best room."

"Go look in the bathroom," I said.

Missy walked back into the bedroom and returned with a big smile on her face. "Nice, very nice! I'm going to call Kim and then unpack," she said.

"Take your time," I told her.

Missy wheeled the suitcase into the bedroom, and I helped her with her shoulder bag. I put it on the king-sized bed and left the room, closing the door behind me. "Thanks," I heard Missy yell from the bathroom.

The other two bedrooms were of equal size. Both had queen-sized beds so I just took the closest one to where I had put down my bag. It didn't take me long to unpack, as I didn't own very much anymore. I grabbed the envelope Marty had given me, sat down on the couch, and emptied the contents out in front of me on the cocktail table. There were menus from four different small restaurants, as well as the number for a service that delivered food from some of the finer restaurants in DC, everything from steak to sushi. Well, at least we wouldn't starve.

I sat and pondered what I should do next. I hadn't thought this whole thing through that far ahead and was sort of winging it. One thing I knew for sure was that Zack was watching me, and I just hoped that he would give me enough time to try to make some changes. If everyone knew what I knew, they would do whatever it took to survive. I just needed to figure out how to make them all believe what I knew to be true. That would be much easier said than done, I was afraid.

Missy came out of the bedroom and walked over to the couch. She was wearing a tiny pair of shorts and T-shirt. I guess she must have noticed I was staring at her. "Should I go put on a robe?" she asked.

54

"No, I'm sorry. It's been a long time since I have been around a woman. I apologize if I made you uncomfortable," I told her.

"Michael, you can look all you like; I don't mind." She laughed. "Now, touching, well, that's a completely different thing." Missy smiled and sat down on the couch a few feet away from me.

"Is it OK if I borrow your laptop? I have some ideas about how to best use the money to help people, but I want to do some research first," Missy asked.

"Sure, be my guest. It's right over there," I said pointing to the case on the dining room table.

"What's all this?" she asked, pointing to the papers I had laid out on the cocktail table.

"They were in the envelope Marty gave me. There is a list of places that will deliver food here. I just started going through it," I told her.

Missy reached over and grabbed the pile of papers. "Is there a grocery store that delivers in this pile?" she asked.

"I don't know. I didn't look through all of it," I replied.

As Missy glanced through the papers, she said, "Yup, there sure is. I usually just eat cereal, yogurt, or fruit for breakfast and have one cup of coffee," she told me.

"There is a deli in there that can deliver breakfast since I doubt the food market can bring us anything by tomorrow morning," I said.

Missy got up from the couch and started looking through the drawers in the kitchen, and then she walked over to the desk in the corner of the living room. It was in there that she found the paper and pens she was looking for. She wrote down something on a sheet of paper and handed it to me. "This is what I'd like for breakfast. If you get up first, you can place the order. If I get up first, I will call it in. Write down what you would like," she told me.

"All right, I will do that before I go to bed," I said.

"I'm beat. I'm going to go do some research on the computer and then hit the sack," Missy said, and she got up from the couch, grabbed the laptop, and walked over behind where I was sitting on the couch. She put her hand on my shoulder, bent over, and kissed my cheek. "Good night, Michael. Thank you for what you did today," she said to me.

"No need to thank me. I'm really glad you're here to help me," I told her. I watched her walk into the bedroom, and I was amazed at how she moved—graceful, yet powerful—and I saw she was so fit that nothing jiggled.

It seems that when Zack turned back the clock for me, making me look and feel like I was thirty again, it had also brought me back to the point where I could get aroused in an instant—though, any man who didn't get excited at the sight of Missy in that outfit needed to have his pulse checked. Not that it mattered. I knew Missy wasn't here because she found me appealing, so I thought it best to put to rest any thought I had of her in that way.

It was getting late, and I was tired, so I wrote down what I wanted for breakfast and headed off to bed. I slept better than I had in a very long time. No dreams that I could recall, and when I looked at the clock, it was ten minutes after nine. I couldn't remember when the last time was that I had slept that late. I put on my robe and walked out of the bedroom. Missy was already there, sitting at the dining room table with my laptop in front of her and papers scattered around the tabletop.

"Good morning," she said.

"Morning," I replied.

"Your breakfast is in the kitchen. I ordered you two coffees, though you will probably have to put them in the microwave to heat them up," she said.

Missy was right; the coffee was not that hot, so I heated it up for a minute; grabbed my bagel, egg, and Canadian bacon sandwich; and joined her at the table. "What's all this?" I asked.

"Well, last night, I got to thinking how to best use the money to help people, and I think it should be used to help the ones who have the least ability to help themselves," Missy said.

"OK, who would that be?" I asked.

"Children and the elderly is what I'm thinking," Missy replied. "There are children going hungry in this country, without food and proper nutrition, Michael. I cannot live with that," she told me.

"All right, you do what you think is best. I have complete confidence that you will make sure the money goes to good use," I told her.

"Thanks, Michael. I just want to make sure it can help as many people as possible," Missy answered. "What are you planning?" she asked.

"Well, it is time for the world to know I am alive," I answered. "I am going to call an old friend at the *Post* and offer her the chance to interview me," I told her.

"What are you going to say?" she asked.

"I have no idea at the moment." I laughed after I answered her. Missy went back to her research, and I finished my breakfast and went in to take a shower. It was strange that I hadn't noticed this before, but my body had now changed as my face had earlier. My muscle structure was different. My belly fat was gone; I was lean and fit again. When I got out and began to shave, I noticed there was no longer hair growing from my ears.

There was a small inconvenience that came along with my new body though. My clothes didn't fit very well and my thirty-four-inch-waist pants were falling off me. I did have a belt with me and used it to keep my pants from falling down. I finished dressing and walked back out to the dining room table where Missy was still sitting. She looked up from her papers at me. I pulled up my shirt to show her what had happened to my body. "I guess I will need some new clothes," I said.

Missy's eyes opened wide as she looked at me. "Holy shit!" she said getting up from her chair. She reached her hand out to touch my stomach but quickly stopped. "Do you mind?" she asked. I shook my head no, and she put her hands on me. "You are pure muscle! There is barely any fat on you anywhere. Did you ever look like this before?"

"No, I never have. I was in better shape when I was younger but never like this," I answered.

"What is going on Michael, why is Zack changing you?" Missy asked.

"I have absolutely no idea why this is happening, but knowing Zack, there must be a good reason for it," I answered.

"Well, you're definitely going to need some new clothes. You look silly in those," she concluded. "I think you ought to make that your first task of the day. If I remember correctly, there is a clothes store about a mile up Wisconsin Avenue. I'll get dressed and go with you," she offered. Missy went into the bedroom, and this time, she didn't close the door. "Do you have any money?" she shouted from the bedroom.

"I have a few thousand in cash in my bag," I replied.

"OK. I'd bring fifteen hundred. You need several things," she replied. I went into my bedroom, took the white envelope out of my bag, and counted what was there. It came out to sixty-two hundred dollars. I took out two thousand and put it in my pocket.

While Missy got ready, I decided to call my friend at the *Post*. Luckily, I still had both her direct line and her cell phone number memorized. I dialed the office number first.

"Sarah Frost, how can I help you?" were her first words when she answered.

"Hello, Sarah, long time," I said.

"Who is this?" Sarah asked.

"You know who this is, Sarah. We sat right next to each other for seven years," I replied.

"Geez, Michael, is this really you?" she asked.

"Yes, Sarah, it's me, and I'm calling for more than just to say hello," I said.

"Should I be afraid to ask what the other reason is?" she asked.

"Well, I don't know. How would you like to interview a dead man?" I asked her.

"You're offering me an interview? Michael, you know the answer to that! My editor would jump at the chance to have Michael Ryan back from the dead and on the front page," Sarah said.

"All right, go talk to him and text me. Can you see the number on your caller ID?" I asked.

"I will right now. How do you want to do this? Should I come to you? I'll need to bring a photographer with me. You know they are going to want pictures," Sarah said.

"No. I'll come to meet you at around two this afternoon. That way, it can make tomorrow's edition. Can you get everything together by then?" I asked.

"For you, Michael, I'm sure I can. I will see you later, and, by the way, I'm glad you're not dead," she said.

"Thanks, Sarah. So am I." I trusted Sarah, but for now, I thought it best not to let too many people know where Missy and I were. Just as I put my phone down, Missy came walking out of her bedroom.

"Was that the reporter you were talking to?" she asked.

"Yes, I'm going to go see her at two this afternoon." Sarah had yet to confirm, but I figured it would take less than ten minutes before she did. After all, I was big news.

"Well then, let's go get you some decent clothes for your photographs," Missy said, grabbing her purse and keys.

I was right. As soon as we pulled out of the underground garage, there was a text message from Sarah confirming our 2:00 p.m. meeting. Missy knew exactly where she was going, and within a few minutes, we were parked in front of what I would call a trendy clothing store.

When I looked around, I really didn't see the type of clothes I was used to wearing, but Missy pointed out that I no longer looked like a fifty-four-year-old man, so I shouldn't be dressing like one. She seemed to delight in picking out the clothes I should buy, and I just let her do it. It turned out my waist was now twenty-nine inches and my chest measured forty-two inches. The shopping trip took about an hour and cost about nineteen hundred dollars, but I had a new wardrobe. "You looked great in those clothes," Missy said as we got back into the car.

"Really? I guess I'm just going to have to get used to not looking my true age," I answered.

"Well, the sales guy sure thought you were looking good. He was eyeing you up big-time," Missy said with a smile on her face.

We drove back to the condo and brought up the bags. "I'm going to put on some of my new clothes," I told Missy and went into the bedroom. I emptied the five bags out on my bed. I had never been much of a clothes guy. A pair of jeans always seemed to work for me. I started looking through the clothes, trying to figure out what I wanted to wear when I heard a knock on the door. "Come on in, Missy," I said.

She opened the door. "Nancy is here." Missy looked over at the bed and at the clothes scattered all over it. As I walked by her, she said, "I'll pick out a good outfit for your interview."

I had only seen Nancy in person a few times, but we had spoken on the phone several times through the years. She was probably around forty, about average height and weight, and she had a very pleasant way about her. "Hi, Nancy, good to see you again," I said reaching out to shake her hand.

"Wow! Marty was right. You do look half your age. It's amazing."

I smiled. "Nancy, this is Missy Franzone." The two women exchanged pleasantries, and Nancy pulled out a large file from the case she was carrying. Then she reached into her pocket and pulled out two credit cards, which she handed to me. I took a look at them. One card had my name and the other Missy's.

"That was fast," I said.

"Marty thought you might need these quickly. As you requested, there is ten million in the account that the cards are attached to. Michael, setting up a charitable trust can take a little while, and Marty thought you might be in a hurry, so he gave me this for you to look over," she said handing me some paperwork.

"OK, I'll look it over. How about what I asked for regarding Missy and her daughter?" I asked.

"It's right here, Michael. I just need to sit down and go over this with Ms. Franzone," Nancy said.

Missy and Nancy sat down at the dining room table, and I decided to go back to my bedroom to find something to wear. I tried on almost everything and found a few things I thought looked good together. Finally, I settled on tan pants and a brown polo shirt. The pants were not what I was used to. They were form fitting, and there was no way the old me could have ever worn them. I walked out of the bedroom and saw that Missy and Nancy were just finishing up.

Missy looked over at me. "Very nice! You look really great in that!"

"I agree, Michael," Nancy added.

"Thank you, Ladies," I replied, and I had to admit I thought I looked pretty good myself.

Missy walked Nancy back toward the front door, and I went over to meet them there. "Nancy, thank you for all of your help," I said.

"No, Michael, we should all be thanking you for what you did and for what you're doing now. I will pray for your success," Nancy said.

"Nancy, wait. Explain the stuff on these papers to me," I said as I walked over to pick them up.

"Marty thought if you wanted to do this quickly, we could just have Miss Franzone choose the charities and entities where you want the money donated and then we would bring the checks over for you to sign. This is the fastest and easiest way to get this done," Nancy told me.

"All right, let's do it that way. Which one of these do I sign?" I asked.

I walked back over to the dining room table and opened up the folder. There were all these little yellow and red "Sign Here" labels sticking out of the sides of the papers. "I guess I'm supposed to sign next to all the stickers," I surmised.

"Yes, Michael," Nancy replied.

I signed in all the designated spots and handed the folder back to Nancy. "Does Missy know what to do in order to get these checks written?" I asked.

"All she needs to do is call me and let me know where the money is going. I'll then prepare the checks for her," Nancy said.

"Well then, I guess we are done. Tell Marty thanks for this," I said as Nancy walked out the front door.

"Oh, I forgot one thing. Marty told me to let you know that you can stay here as long as you need to," Nancy said.

"Thanks again, Nancy. Bye," I said.

"It was nice to meet you, Nancy, and thank you," Missy added.

"You two take care," she replied, her voice trailing off as she walked down the hallway.

I closed the door and walked back over to the dining room table. "So you signed everything you needed to and told them how to get this stuff to your sister?" I asked.

"Yes, Michael, it's done," Missy answered.

"All right, then it's time to head downtown. I think it would be best if you would just drop me off," I told her.

"Why? And if you say for my protection, I am going to slap you upside your head," Missy said.

I could see her starting to get angry. "OK then, we'll go together, but after today, your picture will be everywhere," I said.

She didn't respond; she just grabbed my bag and her car keys and walked toward the front door. "Let's go," she said opening the door.

Chapter Five

Traffic was pretty heavy, and we made it down to Fifteenth Street around one thirty. By the time we found a parking spot and the building, it was a quarter to two. I sent a message to Sarah that we were there and that the woman with me was just giving me a ride and was not part of the story. I knew Missy would have been pissed if she knew I'd done this, but I was going to do whatever I could to protect her. I saw Sarah walking toward us. I put up my hand and gave her a small wave. As Sarah got closer, I could see the expression on her face changing. She had the same look Marty had when he first saw me. Sarah stopped when she got about ten feet in front of us, and she just looked me up and down.

I walked over to her. "It's me, Sarah," I said, seeing the disbelief on her face.

"I don't understand. You look even younger than you did when I first met you twenty-five years ago! We are the same age, Michael. How?" Sarah asked.

"I can't answer that question, Sarah. But it sure is good to see you," I reached out my hand to her. Sarah stepped past my hand and gave me a hug. "So, who is this beautiful lady?" she asked.

Before I could even answer, Missy stepped toward Sarah with her arm extended. "Missy Franzone. It is a pleasure to meet you," she said.

"The pleasure is all mine," Sarah replied. "My editor didn't want to create too much of a stir today, so we're going to use a conference room that is a bit secluded," Sarah said.

I laughed.

"What's funny, Michael?" Missy asked.

"What Sarah is saying is that her editor doesn't want everyone knowing I'm alive until tomorrow's paper comes out. It is all about selling papers, Missy," I explained.

Sarah just smiled and led us to a conference room without any windows. There were two men waiting for us in the room. One was Phil Cramer, the editor of the *Post*; the other I assumed was a photographer.

"Hello, Phil, it's been a long time. How have you been?" I asked, reaching out to shake his hand.

"I've been well, Michael, though by the looks of you, nowhere near as good as you!" he replied. I had known Phil for years. I didn't always agree with his vision of the world or what his idea of good journalism should be, but he was not a bad guy. I was right; the other man in the room was a photographer. "Michael, this is Jerry. He will take your photo and then give me the chip from his camera," Phil told me.

"OK, that's fine with me," I replied.

Jerry reached out to shake my hand, but the whole time, he was ogling Missy. It was so obvious that it was somewhat amusing.

With all the introductions done and Missy refusing to keep her mouth shut and not give Phil and Jerry her name, I thought it was time to set some things straight. "OK, here are the ground rules. I will answer any question you ask as long as it is about Zack or myself. I will not discuss or answer questions about anything else, and you will print everything I say.

Missy's name does not get mentioned, and you will not take any photos of her. Are we all in agreement?" I asked.

All three of them answered with a yes. "All right then, let's get to this," I said. Jerry took a few photos of me and then handed the camera to Phil. Instead of taking out the memory chip, Phil put the camera down on the conference table. "Thanks, Jerry, we'll handle this from here on," Phil said. Jerry just nodded his head and left the room. Missy and I sat down on one side of the table, and Sarah and Phil sat down on the other. Sarah took some papers out of the folder she had in front of her and picked up her hand-held recorder.

"I'm ready. Are you?" Sarah asked.

"Yes, I am," I replied.

"First, I would like to thank you for giving us this exclusive opportunity to speak with you and, on a personal note, I am glad you are still with us," she began.

"Thank you, Sarah. So am I."

"It has been almost a year since the fire destroyed your home and you were presumed dead. Where have you been all that time?"

"Yes, the fire. It did destroy my home, but it was the person who threw the incendiary device through one of my windows that caused the destruction of my home. And also my self-imposed exile from the public eye," I answered.

"But where were you?" she persisted.

"Where I was is not really the issue. The issue is why I am back, don't you think?"

I could see what Sarah was doing. She wanted to know where I had been living so the *Post* could do another story about where I had been hiding and get the neighbors' reactions. She should have started asking about Zack right away; when she didn't, I knew she had other motives. I was not biting, and I think she knew it.

"All right," she said, "so why have you suddenly decided to show yourself?"

"Zack gave me a message, or you could call it a warning, for all of us to either change our ways or suffer the consequences. I think our desire to change might be less than I believed. I think his patience with us is running out."

"So this 'being' you call God is going to destroy us if we do not adhere to his will?"

"You called him God. I call him Zack, and whatever he might be, he does have the power to back up his words. What he is asking us to do isn't so terrible—to stop killing and stop hating, to be decent. Tell me one thing he has asked of us that wouldn't make this world a better place for all of us."

Sarah began to shuffle through the notes in front of her. I had disrupted her rhythm, and she was no longer in control of this interview. I'd been there before in my career, and it wasn't a comfortable place to be. Phil looked over at her, and I could see by the look on his face that he realized what had happened, as well.

"So, this Zack, as you call him, he just wants to help us?" she began again.

"Hasn't he already he cured our diseases? He gave us the truth about ourselves; he gave us a better way to live. What more could we ask for?"

"As you know, there is some debate as to whether any diseases were actually cured long-term," she said.

"Really. Has anyone been diagnosed in the last two years with any of the diseases Zack cured? Please, I think we all know that the only reason anyone debates this issue is because the multibillion-dollar drug companies need sick people to keep turning a profit. But, once again, that is not the reason I am here."

"Are you afraid that the same thing may happen to you again? There are groups out there, like FAD, that view you and this Zack person as a threat, and they had made statements on the Internet condemning you both."

"I don't know who the FAD is, and I am not afraid of a bunch of people who hide behind keyboards spreading messages of hate," I retorted.

"The FAD are Fighters against the Devil, and they are one of many groups who believe that Zack is the devil and you are one of the devil's minions, if not the main one."

I couldn't refrain from breaking out in uncontrolled laughter, and Missy joined me. It took me a couple of minutes to regain my composure, and I had to wipe the tears from my eyes. I felt like asking her to repeat the question just so I could get another belly laugh out of this.

I could see that Phil had told Sarah to sensationalize this. I needed to put an end to that now.

"I really don't care about what the religious community thinks or says or what the drug companies have made people believe. Nor do I care about any of the crackpots who say Zack is an alien or the devil. I am here because most of us chose to ignore his message and his warning, and I, for one, am not going down without a fight. For those who want to join me in that fight, I welcome you. For those who do not, I want you to stay out of the way."

"Fight? What kind of fight are you referring to?"

"Not the kind fought with weapons. The fight I am talking about is the one you wage with love, compassion, understanding, and goodwill toward all mankind. That is what Zack wants from us, and the penalty for not doing so is a price I don't want any of us to pay. No one gets hurt in this fight; in fact, if this fight is won, all of mankind will be the victor."

Sarah looked at me with one of those "you got me" looks. She took her papers and folded them in half. Then she looked over at Phil. Phil just nodded his head, realizing I was not going to let them take me in any direction but my own.

"Well," she said, "what would you have us all do? Remember, Zack warned us of our impending destruction, as well as the cost of our survival. If I remember correctly, the costs were quite high."

"Yes, Sarah, the cost will be high for our survival but nothing compared to our complete destruction. We need to show Zack we can live in peace with each other. All of us need to do that starting right now."

"What about money, Michael? Zack also warned that our new society would be one of equals. How would we live without some form of currency?"

I had no idea how to answer that question, but it did give me the opportunity I was waiting for.

"I don't have all the answers. Remember, I just wrote what I saw and heard. I can do one thing though. I made a great deal of money from the time I spent with Zack, and that money is going to be used to help people. There are still children who go hungry, some even less than a mile from our nation's capital. I don't have enough money to help everyone, but if each one of us who has enough food would help those near their homes who don't have enough, maybe we can all start to feel more human again. We would be helping our fellow man and also proving to Zack that we are worth saving."

Missy grabbed my arm, and I looked over at her. She smiled at me, and there were tears in her eyes. I was on a roll and not done with it yet.

"Oh, yes, and our technology. What great things have we done with it lately? We can kill our enemies or innocent children thousands of miles away with the push of a button. Our technology allows us to breed hate and incubate ideas that we should all be ashamed of. Our technology keeps us from having to interact in person with our fellow man, and we even have our own tech language. Our children get fat and lazy from playing games with handheld devices rather than balls, and every day, our technology takes a little bit more of our humanity away from us. I, for one, will not miss most of it a bit. So, if that is part of the price we have to pay for our survival, well then, I am happy to pay it."

Sarah looked over at Phil. "I think we have what we need, Michael. I want to thank you once again for speaking with us," Phil said.

"Thank you so much, Michael," Sarah added.

Missy and I headed back toward the lobby, and we were about to leave the building when Sarah came running up behind us. "Is there something wrong?" I asked her.

"Michael, what you said in there…is it true? Are we really running out of time?" Sarah asked.

I could see there was a bit of fear in her eyes. "Yes, Sarah, I believe that is very true. I don't know whether we have a day or years left, but I know the clock is ticking and the faster we all start to change, the better," I told her.

"Thank you, Michael. I hope you succeed for all of our sakes," Sarah said and kissed me on the cheek. She hugged Missy before she headed back to her office. Missy and I made our way back to her car, and I waited by the passenger door for Missy to open it.

Instead of opening her door, Missy walked over to me and put her arms around me. "I have never been so proud of anyone as I was of you today. I was right about you, Michael Ryan; you are a good man. You can hug me back, you know."

I wasn't sure what to expect, so I was just standing there with my arms at my side. Then, I put my arms around her and held her. I had never felt a woman's body like hers before. She was solid, and I could feel the contours of her body and the strength in her muscles. It was as if she were carved out of stone in perfect proportions. It felt so wonderful that I could have stood there and held her for hours, but I decided to let go before other thoughts could enter my mind and other parts of my body start to react.

"Thank you, Missy; that means a lot to me," I told her.

Missy smiled at me, and before we parted, she put her right hand on my left cheek and kissed me on the other cheek.

We got back into Missy's car, and as soon as we came out from the underground garage, my phone rang. I looked at the number and recognized it was Marty's. "Hi, Marty. We are just leaving the *Post* now. Everyone is going to know I am alive sometime tomorrow," I said.

"Well, buddy, some people already know you're alive," Marty answered.

"What exactly does that mean?" I asked.

"It looks like someone in my firm decided that they wanted to brown-nose someone in the government, and they gave you up," Marty said. "I am so sorry, Michael. I will find out who did this, and I promise you they will be reprimanded," Marty said.

I could hear the anger in his voice, though I wasn't sure if he was mad because it had exposed me or because he felt someone had violated his firm's client-attorney privilege.

"It's OK, Marty. Like I said, everyone will know I'm alive after tomorrow anyway. Don't bother trying to find out on my account," I told him.

"Michael, you have company. The two of you are being watched. I cannot tell you who it is, probably FBI or NSA, but they are watching you, so be aware," Marty warned.

"All right, but we have no intention of causing any trouble," I told him.

"Oh, one more thing, everything is ready here on my end. Ms. Franzone can call Nancy when she is ready to start giving away the money," Marty said.

"OK, thanks, Marty."

"Good luck, buddy," Marty said before he hung up the phone.

"Is everything OK?" Missy asked me. I told her what Marty had said, and it didn't seem to worry her any more than it worried me.

She was more interested in the fact that they were ready to distribute the money. I kept looking for our tail on the drive back to the condo, but I saw nothing. I was sure what Marty had said was true—that we *were* being watched. At the moment, I didn't know who it was, but I was sure that was the way they wanted it.

Missy looked over at the clock on her dashboard. "We should be back just in time," she said.

"Just in time for what?" I asked.

"Our grocery delivery," she replied.

"Groceries, when did we order groceries?" I asked.

"This morning, right after I ordered breakfast. I called the order in to have it delivered between five and seven. I am not going to eat takeout food every day. It's not healthy, and Zack gave you that amazing body, so you need to start taking care of it," she told me.

"Amazing body" was all I heard of what Missy said. I was feeling good that she had taken notice. "Just so you know, I'm not much of a cook," I admitted.

Missy laughed. "I didn't expect you to cook, Michael; besides, you don't need to cook fruit, yogurt, and cereal," she answered.

73

"Oh, I cannot tell you how excited that makes me," I said sarcastically. "I was kind of in the mood for some sushi tonight. You don't by any chance like sushi, do you, Missy?" I asked.

"I love sushi as long as it's good. There's nothing worse than bad sushi. Let's see if we can find a good place after the groceries come," she answered.

We got back to the condo about fifteen minutes to five, and I searched around for the *Washingtonian* magazine I'd seen when I was checking out the place right after we arrived. I couldn't find it anywhere. "Missy, have you seen the *Washingtonian* magazine?"

"Yes, it's in here; come on in," she answered. I walked in and saw it lying on her bed. "What do you need it for?" she asked as she walked out of the bathroom.

I looked over at her. She was wearing only her underwear. I quickly turned my head away, which Missy seemed to find humorous. "I am not naked, Michael! What are you, some kind of prude or just that much of a gentleman?" she asked.

"Maybe a little of both, Missy. Zack may have made me look like I am thirty and given me this great body, but in my mind, I am still fifty-four years old. I am old enough to be your father, and the fact that I am incredibly attracted to you is still a bit unnerving for me. And, of course, the fact that you look absolutely remarkable in your underwear is not making things any easier," I told her.

"I am sorry, Michael. I hadn't thought about things in that way, but I don't see you as a father figure and you certainly don't look like my father." Missy chuckled as she spoke. "You are a very special man, Michael. I admire what you are trying to do, and I am proud to be here with you," Missy told me. "I am also not unhappy with the fact that you are attracted to me, but we can deal with that at another time."

Luckily, the phone from the lobby started to ring, interrupting our little talk; I was afraid I was going to say something stupid next. Missy grabbed her robe and ran to the phone. It was the front desk asking if we were expecting a delivery. Missy seemed very excited, and she insisted on putting all the groceries away herself. "So what did you want that magazine for?" she asked me after she was done.

"I was going to look for a place to go for sushi," I told her.

"I thought you lived around here for years. Don't you know where to go?" Missy asked.

"Yes, I do, but this is the last night we have before everyone knows I'm alive, and they will know me at BlueFin," I told her.

"Who cares, Michael? Let's just go to the place that has the best food and enjoy," Missy said.

I guess she was right. I would probably be noticed anywhere I went with a tall, gorgeous blonde with me so why not go and eat the best. "All right then, let's go," I said.

We drove to Bluefin, and though they were busy as always, the owner, Yong, took one look at Missy and told his staff to seat us right away. He looked at me and seemed to have no idea who I was, and neither did the rest of the staff. Many of these people had seen me a hundred times or more, but none of them recognized me. *Thanks, Zack,* I thought to myself as they seated us.

As always, the sushi was amazing. They had this way of getting the temperature of the rice perfectly matched with the sushi, and they always used the highest grade of sushi rice. It took me a long time to understand what made good sushi, but after over thirty years of eating it all over the world, I finally understood. The funny thing was that I had never read a food critic's review of a sushi restaurant that was remotely accurate. I doubted any of them had a clue about sushi and the process that went along with doing it right.

When we got back to the condo, Missy wanted to get the list together for the first set of donations. She wanted to make sure she didn't miss anyone. We said our good nights, and I went into my bedroom and lay down on my bed. I began to wonder if I was kidding myself or whether I was having delusions of grandeur. I mean, after all, who was I to think that I had the ability to save mankind, and how was I supposed to make everyone believe that our time was running out?

Zack had yet to show himself, but after what happened tonight, I knew he was watching everything I did. I just didn't understand why he wasn't here with us right now. I knew he had his reasons; he always did. I just wished he would give me some idea of what they were.

I got myself ready for bed, and as I did, I also thought about the beautiful woman who had risked her life to come with me. I knew so little about her, yet I found myself so drawn to her. I had never felt this way about any person before, and the feeling was both unsettling and wonderful. The feelings did not make sense to me, but there was nothing I could do to stop them or control them. I got into bed and fell into a deep sleep within a few minutes.

Chapter Six

I awoke the next morning feeling great and hungry, which was not how I usually felt in the morning. I put on my robe and went out to the kitchen. Missy was already up and had one of her workout outfits on.

"Good morning. Did you sleep well?" she asked.

"Yes, really well," I answered.

"There is creamer in the fridge for coffee, and if you're hungry, there is yogurt and milk for cereal. The cereal is in the cabinet over the sink," Missy said.

I decided on coffee and a strawberry yogurt. I went into the living room and sat down on the couch. Missy came over and sat next to me. "I was waiting for you to get up. I haven't turned on the TV or the radio," she said.

"Well then," I said as I picked up the TV remote, "let's see what the world thinks of my rebirth." I was about to push down the power button but a thought ran through my mind, and I turned to look at Missy. "What about Kim? I think you might need to keep her out of school for a few days. She knows what I look like and may tell people that you're helping me," I told her.

Missy looked at me in a way I had not seen before. She put her hand on my shoulder and looked as if she were going to cry. "Are you all right? Did something happen to Kim or your family?" I asked.

"No, you idiot. I am moved that your first thought was the safety of my daughter, and that means more to me than you can possibly understand. You may be a brilliant writer, Michael, and the one Zack chose, but you know nothing about women and mothers," Missy said, smiling.

I smiled back at her and then chuckled. "Any man who says he knows about women is either lying to the person he is talking to or lying to himself," I said.

Missy laughed. "You got that right!"

I turned on the TV, and it only took a few seconds to see I was the big story. A banner that read, "Michael Ryan Is Alive, Stay Tuned for More Details," was scrolling continuously across the bottom of the screen. I changed the channel, but they were all the same. One anchorwoman held up the day's edition of the *Post*. The headline read, "Michael Ryan Lives." It was too early to know anyone's reaction to the story. I would have to wait until later in the day for that. I turned off the TV and looked at Missy.

"OK, well that part is done. Now comes part two," I said.

"What is part two?" Missy asked.

"Bob Matlin's show," I answered.

"Wait; you mean Bob Matlin, the guy who has that funny news show on cable?" Missy asked.

"Yup, that's the one," I said.

"Why there?" Missy asked.

78

"Bob's show is very popular with that twenty-four-to-thirty-five group everyone talks about. I think it's that age group of people who will be most open to hearing what we need to do in order to make changes in the way we live. It is probably too late for some of the people my age and older. After all, it was many of them who got us to this point in the first place," I said.

"I get your point, but how are you planning to get on the show and where do they film it?" she asked.

"The show is taped in New York, but I am going to pitch them the idea of doing a live broadcast at a studio here in DC," I said. "I've known Bob for about fifteen years. He started out trying to be a journalist, but he found he was better at making people laugh. When he combined comedy with politics, which tend to go very well together, he had a winner. We had talked about my appearing on the show after *Mr. Breeze* came out, but somehow, my schedule and the show's taping never seemed to fit," I explained.

"I'm going to call Nancy and give her the list of places to send the donations. I'm giving away about two hundred million dollars today," Missy said.

"And your reason is?" I asked.

"Michael, you are a controversial figure, and I just want to see how your gifts are received before I go further," she said.

"OK, Missy, you do what you think is best. I'm going to go take a shower and get dressed. Then, I'll watch the news to see how the world is reacting to my return, and I'll give Bob a call," I said.

"OK," Missy said as she walked into her bedroom.

I have to admit, I was feeling a little nervous and scared as well. Zack had not given me a road map or any type of instruction as to how to proceed with all this. In the time I spent with him, he told me only what he wanted me to know when he wanted me to know it. I kept asking myself if this was what he wanted me to do. Right or wrong, I guessed this was the free-will thing Zack was so proud of giving us. I'd decided I was using mine to do what I thought was right.

I showered, shaved, and dressed, and then I went back out to the living room and turned the TV on again. Missy was still in her bedroom as I expected. I had never met a woman who could get herself ready as fast as I could. I remembered Julie used to take forever, and when I would get impatient, she would say, "Beauty takes time."

Wow, Julie! That was someone I hadn't thought about in a long time. I once thought I was in love with her, but Zack was right; I had never loved anything or anyone in my life, and I did not love Julie either. The strange thing was that I found myself fearing for Missy and Kim's safety, and I knew I would die if need be to protect them. I had never put anyone above myself before; nor had I cared enough about any cause to actually do anything but offer an opinion during a conversation. But now here I was trying to save all of mankind. I guessed more than just my appearance had changed.

When I looked at the television screen, I saw what I was waiting to see—public reactions to the announcement that Michael Ryan was alive. As I expected, the feelings went both ways, as they had before I disappeared. Missy came out from her bedroom when she heard the television and sat down next to me. It always struck me as odd, but politicians seemed to have a "no comment" response when it came to either Zack or me. It wasn't that they were all nonbelievers—I was sure some were—but since there was such a great divide in people's thoughts about both Zack and me, none of them could afford to take a public position.

I was encouraged by the fact that almost everyone they asked, who was under the age of thirty-five, had a positive response toward me.

Of course, the change in my appearance brought much speculation. We heard everything from multiple plastic surgeries to the heavens reaching down to cleanse me and—my favorite—the devil comes in many forms.

"It looks like you're going to have your work cut out for you," Missy said, tapping me on the knee.

"Well, fortunately, I don't think I need to have everyone start to change all at once. If that were the case, we might as well kiss all our asses good-bye," I replied.

"I'm going to call Nancy and get these donations rolling. I think you might need all the goodwill this money can buy," Missy said.

I could not argue with that. In fact, the one thing that I hadn't heard mentioned in any of the news reports I listened to was the fact that I was going to use all the money I had made to help those in need. I guess my youthful appearance was more newsworthy than feeding starving children. I had heard enough for now and turned off the television. I found my phone and called Bob's office. His show was called *Pass the Buck*. I had no idea why, but I had to hand it to him, he had quite a loyal following; he had the most watched show on cable TV.

I went through three different people before I got to someone close enough to Bob to relay a message. I told the woman on the phone to tell Bob he should have a gin and tonic at dinner tonight. Bob had gotten so sick on gin and tonic when we were out once that he had sworn to never drink it again.

"Holy shit! If it isn't Michael Ryan. Damn fucking good to hear your voice!" Bob exclaimed.

"Well, it's good to be back among the living," I replied.

"I read the interview you gave the *Post*; it was a teaser piece. When are you planning to tell everyone what's really going on?" Bob asked. Bob was no dummy, and he had great instincts. I was certainly counting on that.

Bob had had a nose for a story back when he was a journalist, and he still did. The difference now was that he had become a showman as well, and any good showman knew you had to entertain your audience to keep them watching. "I'm thinking it's time for me to come on your show," I told him.

"I was hoping you would say that. We have the next four weeks already in the can, but after that would be perfect," Bob said.

"No, Bob, you're not getting the point. I want to go live on your show in two days," I said.

"Michael, we don't do live broadcasts, and how the fuck would you expect me to make this happen in two days?" he asked.

"Well, you know, old friend, those shows you have in the can? If I don't accomplish what I am here to do, there will probably be no one left to watch them," I said.

"All right, I'll make it happen somehow. I'll get back to you in a few hours," Bob said and hung up the phone.

I doubted Bob believed what I said about no one being around to watch the shows he had taped, but I knew if I gave him a line like that, he would be thinking how he could use it to bring in an even bigger audience. Bob and I had another thing in common, our dislike and distrust of the way modern religion was run. I had, in the past, always kept my opinions to myself, whereas Bob had used his to help further his career and to expand his audience.

Personally, I admired his courage. He said what he thought, and he didn't care whom he offended in the process. I also knew he would make this broadcast happen. Like me, he was not the sort of person who gave up until he got what he wanted.

"So how did it go?" Missy asked, walking toward me with papers in her hand.

"Well, I think we might have to make a trip to New York City," I answered.

"Really, hmmm, some great shopping up there," Missy said jokingly.

"How did you do?" I asked her.

"The first batch of checks will be here by noon for you to sign," Missy told me. "When do we need to go to New York?" she asked.

"I'm waiting for Bob to call me back but probably Friday since I'm sure they will want this to run on a weekend night. Missy, do you know where you want to send the rest of the money?" I asked.

"Yes, Michael. I have a list of where I think it will do the most good," she answered.

"Perfect. Please make sure it all gets sent out by the time we're ready to leave for New York," I said.

"OK, it's only Tuesday, so that shouldn't be a problem. Any reason why you want it done so quickly?" Missy asked.

"You've watched Bob's show, right?" I asked.

"Sure," Missy said. "He's funny and very controversial."

"Yes, he is both, and as you know, on his show, he does at times play games with his guests. His bread and butter are the panel discussions, which he uses to pit one side against the other and then make fun of both," I said.

"And?" Missy asked.

"Who do you think they are going to bring on the panel when I go on the show? I can tell you this much; it won't likely be anyone who believes that Zack's words mean what they do to you and me. So I want to be able to use everything possible to show the world that we need to start changing now, and my giving away one point two billion dollars will sure go a long way toward making people believe I'm sincere," I said.

"When you put it that way, I can see your point," Missy said. Our conversation was interrupted by the sound of my phone ringing.

I was surprised; I didn't think even Bob could arrange things so quickly. I picked up my phone and saw the number on the caller ID; it was Marty. "Hi, Marty; what's up?" I asked.

"I read your interview, Michael, nice job. Nancy is leaving in a few minutes to bring the checks for you to sign," he said.

"Thanks, Marty. I appreciate everything you and your firm are doing for us," I said.

"No need to thank me. Besides, you're paying for it," Marty joked. "Listen, one more thing. I'm not sure how this guy found out I represent you, but a detective named Steve Reton called and asked us to pass on his phone number to you. He said he and a few of his buddies were leaving for a vacation to DC today, and he thought maybe he would stop by and say hello," Marty said. "Do you know this guy, Michael?"

"Geez, Marty, did you read a single fucking page of *Mr. Breeze?*" I asked.

"I told you I skimmed through it." Marty answered.

"Detective Reton was involved in the child murder case in San Francisco. I met him when I was traveling with Zack," I said.

"Oh yeah, he tore that guy to pieces; I remember hearing about that," Marty said. "I gave the number to Nancy. It's in the envelope with the checks."

"No, give it to me now if you still have it," I said. Marty gave me the number and then hung up the phone.

Now what is Detective Reton doing here? I wondered. There was some reason for it. I had come to realize that everything that had happened to me in the last two years was part of some plan Zack had. His methods were not always clear, and he sometimes went to great lengths for such small things, like when he drove around the racetrack just to see if he could figure out where the name Mr. Breeze came from. I knew Missy was here for a reason and so was the detective. I just wish I had a fucking clue as to what those reasons were.

Missy was still standing next to me giving me that "what happened?" look. I told her what Marty had said about Detective Reton and that Nancy would be there soon with the checks for me to sign.

"Do you think this means anything, this detective being here?" Missy asked.

"Everything means something, Missy. I just don't have a clue what," I said half smiling.

The doorbell rang, surprising both of us. "I guess Nancy is here already," Missy said, walking over to answer the door.

I could hear two male voices coming from outside the front door, and my first instinct was to grab something to swing.

Missy opened the door and in walked her two brothers. On the right was Tom; the one on the left looked like a slightly older version of him.

"Michael, you already met my brother Tom. This is my older brother Barry," Missy said. I wasn't sure whether I still needed to pick up something to swing at them, but Tom stepped forward and reached out his hand to me. "I'm sorry about what happened before. I didn't know then why my sister was going with you, but I do now. I hope you will accept my apology," Tom said.

"Gladly," I said shaking his hand. I shook hands with Barry, as well. "What are you two doing here?" Missy asked. "Well, we read the interview this morning and thought maybe you two might need someone watching your backs," Barry said.

First, Detective Reton calls, and now Missy's brothers show up. When it came to Zack, I knew better than to believe anything was a coincidence. At first, I was a little taken aback by them just showing up, but then as I thought about it, I realized there must be a reason, so I just decided to go along with it.

"Wow, nice place, Sis," Tom said looking around the condo.

"Please, tell us what we can do to help?" Barry asked me.

"All right, you can help Missy with making sure all the money is donated and she stays safe when we leave for New York on Friday," I said.

Barry and Tom looked at each other and then back at me. "We can do that," they both answered almost in unison.

Missy gave me a funny look and walked over to me. "Barry, Tom, could you excuse us for a moment?" she said as she led me into her bedroom and closed the door. "What is going on, Michael?"

"What do you mean?" I answered.

"Come on, Michael; I realize we haven't known each other very long, but somehow, I can sense what you're feeling and I sense that you're worried," she told me.

I was worried. I had decided what my next move would be after appearing on Bob's show, and the timing of her brothers' arrival and the phone call was making me uneasy.

"All right, here goes. I woke up this morning, and I realized what we have to do next after I go on Bob's show. First, Marty calls and tells me Detective Reton is here in DC, and then your brothers show up—"

"Wait a second; what do you mean 'what we are doing next'? You never said anything to me about what we are going to do next," Missy said interrupting me midsentence.

"No, I never got the chance to," I replied.

"So what is next?" Missy asked impatiently.

"I'm going to use Bob's show to announce that I want to have a rally on the Mall a week from tomorrow. I want everyone who believes we need to be better human beings to come together and be counted. I want to urge people in every corner of the world to join together and show that they believe we have the ability to change," I said. "I have been winging this from the beginning, Missy, or at least I thought I was, but what happened this morning tells me we are going to need protection, and Zack is sending it to us," I said.

Missy looked at me like she somehow knew what I was thinking. "Do not even suggest to me that I should leave, Michael. I'm not going anywhere," she said with anger in her voice.

"No, you are not, but your brothers are," I said.

"Why? You just said we may need protection," Missy said.

"We do, and I'm going to call Detective Reton. I bet his friends are police as well, and your brothers are going to have to go back home and make sure Kim and your sister Ann are safe," I said.

Missy stopped giving me her menacing look and smiled. "I guess I didn't know what you were thinking after all. I'll go tell my brothers. Thank you, Michael. Thank you for thinking of Kim and my sister," Missy said and kissed me on the cheek before she left the bedroom to go speak with her brothers.

I waited about ten minutes before I left the bedroom. When I walked into the living room, Missy and her brothers were saying their good-byes. "Are you sure you don't want us to stay?" Barry asked me.

"No, Barry, we'll be OK. Missy will feel much better if you two are there to watch out for Kim and Ann," I said.

"All right, you two be careful," Barry said.

I shook both their hands as they left the condo. "OK, now that they're gone, spill it, Michael. What made you change your mind about Barry and Tom staying here to help?" Missy asked.

Not much got past Missy, and I guess I should have expected I would have to give her a better explanation than I had earlier. "Don't ask me how I know this, but this feeling came over me that your brothers should be with Kim and Ann and not us. I can't tell you why; I just knew it was the right thing to do," I said.

Missy seemed to accept my reason. "All right, then I think you should call that detective if we are going to need protection. It might be nice to actually have it around," Missy said.

I wasn't about to argue that point. I picked up my phone and went to find the paper with Detective Reton's phone number.

Chapter Seven

I dialed the phone number Marty had given me, and a man's voice answered. It had been awhile since I'd seen Detective Reton, and I didn't know him well enough to recognize his voice. "Is this Detective Reton?" I asked.

"Yes, it is, Michael Ryan, and please call me Steve," he answered.

"All right, Steve, is there something I can do for you?" I asked. I was pretty sure I knew why he was calling, but I wanted him to tell me. "Look, Michael, my buddies and I read your interview, and we know what you're trying to do. We also know about the loonies that tried to kill you last time. We want to make sure that doesn't happen again, so, like it or not, we are on our way to DC to watch your back," he said.

"Thank you, Steve, and your help is more than welcome and greatly appreciated," I said. "Where are you now?"

"We're in Chicago. Our flight for DC leaves in an hour. We'll arrive this afternoon around three," Steve said.

"We? How many of you are there?" I asked.

"Including me, six. All officers who remember what they saw that day. Michael, all of us had someone who had an incurable disease that they no longer have. We all know who Zack is, Michael, and we all have seen enough scum to last ten lifetimes. We believe in what you're trying to do," Steve said.

"Well, let's hope I can convince more people to feel the way you do. Listen; let me work on a place for all of you to stay. Call me at this number when you land. I'll also arrange for you to be picked up from the airport," I said.

"OK, thanks, Michael. I'll let the guys know," Steve said.

"No, Steve, thank you, to all of you," I said and hung up the phone.

Missy was standing next to me waiting for me to tell her what the detective had said. "So?" she asked impatiently.

I gave her my best devilish smile and told her the details of the conversation.

"You were right," Missy said.

"Yes, I was. Now I want you to call your sister and let her know your brothers are coming. Ask her to go to your house and pick up anything Kim will need for the next ten days, *and tell her she is not to go back to your house for any reason after today*," I said. I thought for sure Missy was going to ask me why, what, and how, after I said that, but she just went to find her phone and called her sister. While she was talking, the doorbell rang. I looked out the peephole and saw it was Nancy. I let her in.

"Good morning, Nancy," I said.

"Good morning to you, Michael," Nancy replied, as she handed me the envelope that contained the checks.

I heard Missy say good-bye to her sister as she came walking into the living room. "Hi, Nancy. Can I talk to you for a minute?" she asked.

"Sure," Nancy answered and followed Missy into the kitchen. I opened the envelope, signed the checks, and waited for the two of them to finish talking. It didn't take long.

Missy led Nancy back to the front door. "Nancy, please make sure the checks to these charities are sent overnight, and tell Marty I need to speak with him as soon as he is available," I told her.

"Of course, Michael," Nancy said as she walked out the front door.

"What do you need me to do?" Missy asked.

"I am glad you asked because we do need to do a few things. First, there is a Marriot in Bethesda. I need you to call them or go there, whichever you prefer, and rent a floor, if possible. If not, get six rooms that are close together. Then, we'll need a limo to pick up Steve and his men at the airport and bring them to the hotel, and, lastly, we will need two limos to get us to New York on Friday," I told her.

"OK. I'm so glad I asked. And what are you going to be doing while I'm getting all this done?" Missy asked and smiled at me.

"Well, hopefully, I'll be getting us a permit so we can have our rally next week, and then I'll make sure we have a place to stay in New York and a reason to go there to begin with," I told her.

"I think I'll take a ride over to the hotel. I have a craving for Chinese food. I'm going to pick up some takeout for lunch. Do you want something?" Missy asked.

Chinese food sounded good to me. "Sure, I'll have some roast pork with Chinese vegetables and please ask them to go light on the sauce. I hate when they smother it in so much sauce you can't even taste the food," I replied.

Missy grabbed her bag and keys and headed for the front door.

"Good luck," I told her.

"You too, Michael," Missy said walking out the door.

As much as I liked Missy's company, I was glad for the opportunity to be alone. I was feeling a little better about myself and my chances of success after what had transpired this morning. I knew Zack was watching every move I made, and when needed, he was giving me a sign that I was moving in the right direction. My thoughts were interrupted by the sound of my phone ringing. It was Marty calling. I assumed Nancy had given him my message.

"Hey, Marty," I said answering the phone.

"So, what's so important?" he asked.

"Who issues permits for a rally on the National Mall?" I asked.

"Hold on," Marty said. I didn't think he would know the answer off the top of his head. "The National Mall and Memorial Parks Division of Permits Management. Why do you ask?" Marty replied.

"I need a permit for a rally that will be held one week from tomorrow," I said.

I could hear Marty start to chuckle. "Michael, buddy, look I have been very supportive of you and your quest, but come on, what the fuck are you doing?" he asked. "First, you show up after a year during which time I never heard from you unless you needed money sent to you," he added. "And now you come to me with this woman and this story that we are about to be wiped off the face of the Earth by this Zack, who, by the way, has not fucking been seen or heard of since that day in Ohio when you were shot. Look, I'm just laying out the facts here, and the facts are that your guy Zack either doesn't seem to care what we do to each other or he is gone and is not coming back," Marty said.

I sat there and thought for a moment. How was I supposed to convince a bunch of strangers about Zack when I couldn't even convince people who knew me.

"Marty, are you telling me that you don't believe anything I told you about the dream I had or about seeing Rover again?" I asked.

"Michael, what have you been doing for the last year? If I remember correctly, you were getting stoned every day and listening to nothing but the Grateful Dead. Don't you think that that may have had some effect on your state of mind?" Marty asked. "I'm not saying you're lying, Michael, but you have to understand how hard all of this is to swallow. I'm sure you had the dream—hey, I'm sure you had lots of dreams over the past year. As far as the ten-foot-tall German shepherd that is smarter than any of us and also has the power to destroy us, well, I'm still not sure if I can buy into that one," he said. "And this woman with you. Michael, have you really looked at her? I don't think I've ever seen a woman that remarkably gorgeous in my life. And she meets you, drops her whole life, leaves her daughter with her sister to follow you around. Someone she has known for—what?—a fucking week! Please, Michael, wake the hell up. The Michael Ryan I knew would have never taken anything at face value. He would look at every angle and peek under every rock to find out the real story, and he would have never accepted that someone would just stop her life to follow a stranger around," he concluded.

Marty was right, but I was no longer the man he used to know—hell, I was no longer the man I used to know. I never cared about anything but myself, and now I seemed to care about everyone, especially Missy and her daughter, Kim. I also knew that I wasn't going to be able to make everyone believe what I was saying, and it looked like Marty was a lost cause too.

"You're not wrong in your thoughts, Marty. I can see how it might look to you, but you are wrong about my state of mind. You are very wrong about Missy. If you don't want to help me any further, I understand," I told him.

"Michael, I didn't say I wasn't going to help you. I am just trying to make you see that what you're doing and saying sounds crazy. I also have to admit the fact that you might be right scares the crap out of me," he said.

93

"You know, Marty, I didn't ask for any of this and nothing has been the same in my life ever since I saw that first story about Zack over two years ago. I know you only skimmed through *Mr. Breeze*, but did you happen to read the part where Zack told me what would happen if I decided not to fucking write *Mr. Breeze?*" I said, raising my voice.

The other end of the line was silent for about forty seconds. "All right, Michael, I read the book. In fact, I read it twice. The truth is everyone I know, including those in the government, read the book. The fact is also that I don't know anyone who didn't read it. So, yes, I know you didn't have much of a choice," he said.

"Look, Marty, I have to do this. Just so you know, when I look in the mirror these days, I don't see the man I used to be looking back at me, and at times, I do miss that uncaring, single-minded son of a bitch, but the man I've become knows what he must do and whether I like it or not, it seems it's up to me to save us.

"So I am going to do whatever I can to accomplish that goal, and if I piss off some folks along the way, so be it. Are you going to help me or not? For the moment, that is all I need to know," I said.

"Yes, Michael, I'll do whatever I can to help, but a permit in a week might be a stretch even for me," he answered. "Is there anything else you need besides the permit?"

"No, we can handle the rest from here. Thanks. I know this is causing you and your firm problems," I said.

"Well, Michael, I am very sure that this is nothing compared to the problems we'll have if you fail. I'll be in touch," he said and hung up the phone.

Somehow, I felt relieved by Marty's confession that he had read *Mr. Breeze* and that everyone he knew had read it as well. I sat and thought about that night in Nashville when I first met Zack and all the time I spent with him.

Did anything that happened during that whole time occur by chance, or was it one big play with Zack directing the characters for me to witness? Zack told me I was chosen because I was different. I had never believed in anything, ever. I never questioned that, and that had always eaten at me. There must have been thousands of nonbelievers out there, and I was sure more than a few of them could have relayed Zack's message. I had learned that Zack only gave the answers he wanted to give, and those answers were never complete. There was always more to what he said. I wondered what the "more" was when it came to my purpose, since I was sure he wasn't done with me yet.

Once again, my thoughts were interrupted by the sound of my phone ringing. It was Bob calling me back. "So, do you have news for me?" I asked when I answered the phone.

"Sure do! We're going live Friday night at seven, and I need you here by five. Am I amazing or what?" Bob answered.

"You are," I answered.

"What is your email address? The producers need to send you a bunch of stuff, and I told them they didn't have to pay you to come on the show," Bob said.

I laughed and gave him my email address. "Bob, thanks for getting this done; you have really helped me out," I said.

"No problem. We're going to have a great show, maybe the best one yet," he replied.

"I'll see you Friday," I said.

"Michael, you be careful and watch your back. They are bringing in extra security for Friday since you are the loony-tune people's poster boy, but, in your case, they've got a target painted on you. You might want to have a look around online and see what's going on, especially with the FAD.

Those fuckers really seem to have a problem with you still breathing. You also might want to get yourself some security of your own," he suggested.

"Thanks, Bob. I have some people on their way here to handle the security, and I already checked out the FAD," I answered.

I went to get my laptop and began to search around the web. There were some positive things said about my interview with the *Post*, but for the most part, the comments went from nasty to threatening. I found the FAD webpage and discovered Bob was right about this group. They called themselves Fighters against the Devil, but it appeared in their minds, the devil took many forms. The devil was black; the devil was Jewish; the devil was not American; and the devil was anyone that they thought should not be allowed to exist. In other words, they were equal-opportunity haters.

It seemed Bob was right. I was on their home page, and there was a target on my forehead. Then I saw something that really pissed me off. There was a picture of Missy on their website as well. They didn't have her name listed, but there was also a target on her forehead. I clicked on the photo of Missy to see if I could enlarge it for more detail, and when I did, I could see the photo had been taken when she was standing outside of the *Post's* building. Someone knew we were going to be there. I guess Sarah had not been as careful as she thought she was. I was right to send Missy's brothers back to watch over Kim and Ann. It wouldn't take long for them to attach a name to her face.

The more I looked around on the web, the more hate I saw. I started to wonder if maybe Zack was right about what we had allowed our technology to do to our humanity. I heard the front door open and looked up. Missy was back, and I could smell the Chinese food that was in the brown paper bag she was carrying. Missy looked at my face and could tell there was something wrong.

"What is it Michael?" she asked.

I showed her what I had found on FAD's website. "You need to call your brothers and your sister now, Missy. Once they find out who you are, it won't take them long to find out about Kim and your family," I warned.

"Those motherfuckers. They better not bring Kim into this, or I swear, Michael, I will find them and beat them with whatever I can find," Missy said with an anger I had not seen in her before. "What do you think I should tell them?" Missy asked.

"Will you listen and just do what I tell you to do?" I asked.

"Yes, I promise," Missy answered.

"Good, because this time, you need to put aside your stubborn, independent streak and listen. First, call Ann and have her keep Kim out of school for the rest of this week and all of next week. Then, call your brothers and tell them what is going on. I'm sure Ann and Kim can stay with one of them, but let them know things are going to get worse."

"These people are fanatics, Missy; they aren't fighting against the devil. They are a hate group just using the devil bullshit as an excuse to label anyone who they think should not be allowed to live as a servant of the devil."

"All right, Michael. I'll call right now," Missy said, picking up her phone.

I sat there and listened as Missy called her sister and her brothers, as well as her parents and her sister Joan, warning them of what might happen.

I could see the look of concern and anger on her face as she spoke to each of them. Missy put the phone down on the cocktail table and sat down on the couch next to me. "How did you know?" she asked me.

I knew what she was thinking. She thought I had some forewarning of what would happen and that was why I sent her brothers away. "It was only a hunch, but I knew it wouldn't take long for the people who failed to finish the job last time to resurface, and I knew anyone around me would become a target, as well," I answered.

Missy looked at me, put her arm around my shoulder, and kissed my cheek. "You keep surprising me, Michael Ryan," she said.

97

I'll admit I didn't know what she meant, but since Missy was giving me a compliment, I decided to not question it. "So, how did you do on your little outing?" I asked.

"Well, we have secured the entire fifth floor at the Marriot, and the hotel will take care of the limos, as well. I instructed them to be at the airport at three," Missy replied. "And, of course, I brought back lunch," she added. "So, what have you been doing while I was gone besides missing me?" Missy asked smiling.

"Well, I had a pretty intense conversation with Marty," I answered.

"I get this feeling he doesn't like me very much. Does he have a problem with women?" Missy asked.

"It isn't you. He is scared, and like most proud men, instead of showing his fear, he shows anger; it has nothing to do with you. After all, he doesn't know you, Missy. If he did, he couldn't help but like you," I said.

Missy smiled. She seemed to accept my explanation.

"But the big news is that we're going to New York and I'm appearing on Bob's show, which will be live. We go on at seven, but we need to be there by five," I told her.

Missy's eyes lit up. "Nice, but why do I think there is a 'but' in there somewhere?" she asked.

"Well, let's eat lunch, and I'll tell you the rest," I said.

We ate our lunch, which was really good. I didn't realize how much I had missed real Chinese food. The only kind I had eaten over the last year came out of a microwave. I told Missy what Marty had explained to me about the permit for the rally and also what Bob had said about the added security measures that were being taken.

"So, can you have the rally without the permit?" Missy asked.

"Technically, I would think not. But, regardless, I am going to announce it on Bob's show," I answered.

"And what about these wackos? Are they really that dangerous?" Missy asked.

"I've done stories before on people like the FAD, and they are breeders of hate. They aren't usually the ones you need to watch out for, but there are those who teeter on the edge of sanity and when they begin to identify with that message of hate, well then, you have a problem. And in the high-tech world we now live in, that message of hate is delivered at lightning speed, and it can spread everywhere in a matter of seconds," I replied.

"So, are you saying we need to be worried or not?" Missy asked.

"Believe me; we do need to be worried, and I think before the day is over, they will have a name to go along with your picture," I told her.

"Why are you doing this, Michael? You are giving your money away; you are risking your life trying to save people, many of whom would like nothing more than to see you dead. Why are you really doing this?" she asked.

I sat there for a moment with my chin on my chest trying to come up with a good answer to her question, but somehow, nothing came to my mind. "I really wish I could give you an answer to that question, Missy, but I can't. I just know that it is something I have to do, and if I don't make it through this, well then, so be it, but I'm not giving up.

"Zack is watching everything we're doing, and I somehow know that when we really need him, he will come," I said.

"Well, I hope you're right about that, Michael, for both our sakes," Missy said, getting up from the couch. "I've got a lot of money to give away before Friday," she added as she sat down at the table and began to look at the papers scattered in front of her.

"Missy, can I ask you to handle one more thing for me?" I asked.

"Sure, Michael; what is it?" Missy replied.

"We're going to need transportation to and from New York on Friday. I figure two limos would work unless they have one big enough to fit all eight of us comfortably," I said.

"We aren't spending the night?" Missy asked.

"I think it would be better for us if we returned here right after the show. We have to start to plan for the rally, and I also think it would be safer for us both if we came back, rather than stay the night in New York," I said.

I saw the look on Missy's face after I told her we would be coming back here. She looked disappointed. "I'm sorry; I know you wanted to spend some time in New York."

"Michael, I was kidding about the shopping thing. I couldn't care less about that. I miss Kim, Michael. This is the first time I've ever been away from her. We have never been apart, and I just miss her. I know you can't possibly understand what I'm feeling since you've never had children," she said.

"I am sorry—" I was saying as Missy cut me off midsentence.

"Don't you dare say you're sorry you brought me along. Michael, I am a big girl, and I am here because it was my choice to be here. So just let me miss my daughter. You don't need to say anything more about it," Missy said defiantly.

"OK, conversation over," I said holding my hands up in surrender. Missy was right; I didn't know what it felt like to miss someone. Hell, I didn't even know what it felt like to love someone—though lately, I had started to feel something that I had never felt before.

It might seem like a normal feeling for most people, but it was a new one for me. For the first time in my life, I wanted someone to be around me, to be near me. In the past, after spending a few hours maximum with someone,

I couldn't wait to be alone again. I was always finding some excuse to escape, but with Missy, it was different. I wanted her with me as much as possible.

I heard my phone ring. I saw the number and knew Detective Reton had arrived in DC. "Hello, Detective; how was your flight?" I asked.

"It was fine, and please call me Steve. I'm not on the clock out here," he answered.

"All right, Steve, there is a car waiting for you. It will take you to the hotel, which is not far from where we are staying. Once you get settled in, give me a call, and I will give you our address," I said.

"*Our* Address?" Steve asked.

"Yes, Steve, our. I'll explain when I see you," I answered. I heard a beeping sound from my phone. Another call was coming through, so I looked at the number. It was Marty. "Well, I didn't expect to hear back from you so soon," I said.

"I'm sorry I lost my cool with you before, Michael. I know what you're trying to do, and I know you and your friend are risking your lives to accomplish it," Marty said.

"Marty, it's OK. Thanks for calling to tell me that, but I'm not upset with you," I said.

"Well, that's not the only reason I'm calling you. They didn't waste much time. They're already talking about you appearing on Matlin's show, and it might take some doing to get you that permit for your rally at the Mall," Marty said.

"Why?" I asked.

"You're having—by their definition—a demonstration, and that means you need a public gathering permit, and those take a little longer to get. They usually also ask you to come in and speak with them," Marty answered.

"Marty, I know how much influence you have. Can't you pull a few strings?" I asked.

"Might not be that simple, buddy. Religious groups have a huge lobbying machine in this town, and I can tell you they're already starting to mobilize, but, so far, you haven't said anything that threatens them, so they're holding back. However, once you announce this rally, well, things might change pretty fast," he told me.

"All right Marty, but I'm going to announce this rally on Friday night, regardless. I don't know what will happen if they don't grant the permit, so please do what you can," I said.

"What was that all about?" Missy asked after I put the phone down. I told her about my conversation with Marty and that we were going to go ahead with our plan regardless of whether or not we got the permit by Friday. I didn't know if Missy agreed with my decision, but I think she knew there was no changing my mind, so she didn't try. "OK, whatever you think is best," she said and went back to work on the donations.

When I heard my phone ringing once again, I knew it was Steve Reton calling to let me know they had arrived at the hotel.

"Hi, Steve, are you guys all settled in?" I asked.

"Yes, and thanks for doing all this for us. This is a nice place, and you really didn't need to have a limo for us, Michael; in fact, I want to talk to you about that," Steve replied.

"Limos are no good?" I asked. I didn't know exactly what he was trying to tell me.

"Michael, if we are going to protect you, we need to do it our way. So no more limos for us; it attracts too much attention," Steve told me.

"OK, what do you want me to do? What do you need?" I asked.

"First off, where are you? I think we need a face-to-face meeting so you can meet the guys and we can explain how this will work best," Steve said.

"All right, when do you want to meet?" I asked.

"Now," Steve replied.

I gave Steve our address and hung up the phone. "That was Detective Reton. He and his friends are on their way, and they want to talk to us about some things. They didn't like my limo idea," I said to Missy.

About fifteen minutes passed before we heard a knock. I walked over and opened the door. "Why didn't you ask who it was?" were Steve's first words to me.

"Well, I knew you guys were on your way and I assumed it was you," I answered.

"Michael, you need to stop assuming things if we are going to prot—" Steve stopped midsentence when he saw Missy walk into the room.

I looked back at Missy and then to Steve and the men with him. They were all looking at her, their eyes moving up and down her body. Missy must have sensed this as well, since she came to my side and put her arm around my waist, in a gesture I knew was meant to let them know that she was taken. "This is Missy. Now why don't we all go sit down, and you can tell me what your ideas are," I said. Steve introduced all of the men with him, and we went into the living room and sat. Missy made sure she was on the end of the couch right next to me.

"Look, Michael, if we are going to protect you, we need to do it our way," Steve said.

"What exactly does that mean, Steve?" I asked.

He handed me a piece of paper. I looked at it, and there were names of several companies on it. "What's this?" I asked.

"These are names of security companies that specialize in protecting dignitaries. They have drivers trained in tactics that could keep you alive, as well as the vehicles we would like to use," Steve said.

"All right, Steve, you contact whomever you want and get what you think is best, but let me explain something to all of you. We are going to New York on Friday, and I will announce my plans to hold a rally on the following Wednesday at the National Mall. All you need to do is keep me in one piece until then. You can use the phones here to contact whomever you want, and if they need payment, either Missy or I will take care of that," I said.

Steve handed the piece of paper he had shown me to the man next to him and told him to make it happen. I got up off the couch taking Missy by the hand. I led her into the bedroom, closing the door behind me.

"What's the matter?" she asked.

"In a few minutes, Steve is going to knock on this door and tell us there is no way the six of them can protect us at an outdoor rally with that many people and in that large an area. I know he is right, but I also know that we will be safe from harm. I have no reason other than that I cannot believe Zack would let anything happen to us. Are you with me on this?" I asked.

Missy put her arms around my neck and hugged me. "Yes, Michael, I am with you," she said.

We heard the knock on the bedroom door. "Come in," I said.

As expected, it was Steve. "Look, Michael, I get what you're trying to do, but getting yourself killed is not going to help anybody. These crazies are not really that organized, so you two are probably safe until we get to New York. I don't know if you are aware of it, but there are two cars parked outside with federal agents watching the building," he said.

"I know about the agents, Steve, and we are both grateful you guys are here. I know it will be almost impossible to protect us at the rally, but I have to go through with it.

"You see, I'm not picking out who I'm trying to save. I'm trying to save all of us, including the people who would love it if I were dead," I said.

"All right, I had to try even though I didn't think I'd be able to change your mind. Do you remember that day in the alley, Michael?" Steve asked.

"Yes, I will never forget that," I answered.

"You carried that little girl out of that alley, and you handed her to her mother and then you tried to go back down the alley," Steve said. "I could see it in your eyes you had no fear you were determined to do what you thought was the right thing with no regard for your own safety."

"Yes," I answered.

"Well, I knew right then that you were either brave, stubborn, or crazy, and I'm still trying to figure out what combination of those three you are," Steve said smiling.

"When you figure it out, please let me know," I replied jokingly.

Steve gave us a half-cocked smile and walked out of the bedroom.

I followed Steve back out into the living room. He once again introduced me to all of the men with him. Each one seemed to have his own specific duties. Frank was handling the transportation, and once he completed his part of the call, he handed me the phone and I gave the company my payment information. I noticed two of the men were no longer in the condo. When I asked where they were, Steve told me they were going to check out the building to see how easy it would be for someone to get in.

"Michael, come here." Steve motioned to me with his hand as he called out. "Have a look," he said pointing to the tablet screen. I hadn't even noticed they had brought that tablet in with them. It was FAD's website, and it appeared it didn't take them long to find out Missy's name; in fact, they had even listed her address under her name.

"Can I borrow that?" I asked.

Steve handed me the tablet, and I went back into the bedroom. Missy was talking on her phone. I realized she was talking to Kim so I sat down on the bed and waited for her to finish her conversation. I didn't want to upset her while she was talking to her daughter. It turned out she could tell by the look on my face that something was wrong.

"What's the matter?" Missy asked after she ended her call.

I handed her the tablet. "Have a look," I said. Missy looked at the tablet, and she grabbed hold of my forearm. Without saying a word to me, she picked up her phone. "Ann, are Barry and Tom with you?" she asked. I was only able to hear one side of the conversation. Missy saw that, and she handed me her phone. "It's my brother, Barry," she said.

"Barry, listen. The FAD has posted Missy's picture on their website with a target on her forehead. They now have her name and address posted under the picture," I said.

"Understood. What do you want us to do?" Barry asked.

"Please stay away from Missy's house, and don't let Kim go to school," I answered.

"Understood. How about the two of you. Are you safe where you are?" Barry asked.

"Yes, we have a small army here with us, and the government has cars out front watching over us as well," I replied.

"Good, may I speak with my sister, please?" he asked.

I handed the phone back to Missy, and she said her good-byes and then ended the call.

"Are you all right?" I asked.

"Yes, Michael, I'm OK," Missy answered.

I picked up the tablet, and Missy and I went back into the living room.

Chapter Eight

"So, what do you want us to do?" I asked Steve while handing him the tablet.

"Well, first of all, neither of you should exit this building until we leave for New York on Friday. By now, your government guard dogs have already gotten back IDs on the photos they took of us when we entered the building, and I'm sure they're tracking your credit cards, as well," Steve said.

"Well, I think we can stay inside for a couple of days, so that shouldn't be a problem. What else?" I asked.

"I noticed you have an empty bedroom. I would like for one of us to stay here with you. Also, we will keep an eye on the building and on your guard dogs out there," he said.

I looked over at Missy, and I could see by the look on her face she was not pleased with having someone stay here. "Will you guys excuse us for a moment?" I asked, getting up from the couch and reaching my hand out to Missy. She took my hand, and we walked into the bedroom.

"You aren't thrilled with one of them staying here, are you?" I asked.

"You know, Michael, I haven't lived with a man in a long time. For some reason I can't explain, I'm comfortable with you, but these guys kind of creep me out," Missy told me.

"Michael, I think you should come in here now!" I heard Steve shout. Missy and I looked at each other, and I was about to continue our talk when we heard Steve again. "Michael, you really need to come in here now!" I opened the door. Steve and his men were all backed up against the wall of the condo. Rover was standing in the middle of the room. The ceilings of the condo were nine feet tall, and Rover's ears brushed up against them as he turned his head to look at Missy and me.

"Holy shit!" Missy said. I used my arm to move Missy behind me.

"Let's all be still. He understands everything you say, so no one is to speak but me. Understood?" I said. I looked around. Steve and all his men nodded their heads in acknowledgment.

"Hello, Rover! I know you can understand me, but I can't understand you, so can you nod your head, yes or no, if I ask you questions?" I asked. Rover nodded in agreement. "Did Zack send you to watch over us?" I asked. Rover nodded yes. I guess Rover had other ideas about how we could communicate. He turned his head toward one of the walls of the condo, and a large screen appeared before our eyes. The message, "Hello, Michael and Missy," was written on it.

"Hello, Rover," Missy said "Wow, this is pretty cool," she added.

"What is it Rover? Why are you here?" I asked. The answer to my question began to appear on the screen. "I am always watching you. No one else needs to be in this place but the two of you," was the reply. I didn't know why there would be a problem with one of these men staying there, but I knew I wouldn't get an answer even if I asked.

"All right, Rover. Is it OK if they stay outside and watch the building and help us get to New York and through the rally safely?" I asked.

"Yes," appeared on the screen.

"OK, we will abide by your wishes," I said.

Rover looked at me and then turned his head to look at Missy, who was still halfway hiding behind me. "Do you want to see Missy?" I asked. Missy didn't wait for Rover to reply. She stepped out from behind me and slowly walked toward him, stopping a few feet away from him.

She tilted her face upward so she could see his head. Rover looked down at her, staring into her eyes. I walked over to Missy's side. A smile came to her face, and tears began to run down her cheeks. She put her hand up and touched the side of Rover's head. "Thank you," she said trying to hold back her tears. Rover looked over at me and nodded his head up and down. I could swear he smiled at me, and then he disappeared.

"Holy fuck!" one of Steve's men yelled out. I put my hand on Missy's shoulder.

"Are you all right?" I asked.

"Yes, I am, Michael. For the first time in a very long time, I am," Missy answered.

"What happened?" I asked.

"He took my anger away, Michael. When he did, what I should have felt years ago when Steve died, finally came through. He let me feel grief and loss instead of the hunger for revenge and the hatred that had taken away any chance I ever had to feel joy again. It is much more than that, but I can't find the words to explain it any better," Missy answered. I didn't know exactly how to respond to her so I put my arms around her and held her close to me. Missy's body seemed to relax and melt into mine—a far different feeling than the tenseness I had felt through her body every time I had been close to her before.

"Steve, I think it's best that we stay here alone. Do what you need to keep the building as secure as possible and whatever else you can to keep us safe until the rally," I said, not letting go of Missy.

"You got it, Michael. Let's get going, guys; we have work to do," Steve said, motioning for the men to follow him. When I heard the front door close, I let go of Missy, and we sat down together on the couch.

"Zack is God, Michael; I know that now. There is no longer any doubt in my mind," Missy said, tears still rolling down her cheeks.

I got up from the couch and brought her back some tissues to wipe her eyes. I looked at her and smiled. "Yes, he is, Missy, and his reasons for doing things are beyond my understanding, but I know if need be, he can be a very vengeful god," I answered.

"The Old Testament! Michael Ryan, I thought you were an unbeliever," Missy replied with a smile.

"You don't need to be a believer to be curious, and, yes, I have read my share of religious books," I replied, smiling back at her.

"It looks like we'll be stuck here for a couple days. Let's make the most of it. I will help you choose where to send the rest of the money, and we can relax a bit since I think things are going to get pretty crazy, starting Friday," I said.

"Well, we'll make it work. Excuse me; I am going to go call Kim. After what just happened I need to hear her voice. I'll be back in a few minutes," Missy said.

"OK," I replied.

Missy started to walk toward the bedroom but then suddenly stopped, turned around, and looked at me. "Would you like to say hello to Kim?" Missy asked me.

I'll admit I was taken aback a bit by her question, but I blurted out, "Sure." Missy gave me a big smile and continued to walk into her bedroom but only stayed in there long enough to grab her phone. I listened to her talk to her daughter, and for the first time in my life, I wasn't thinking to myself that I was glad I didn't have kids to deal with.

Instead, I was thinking how sad it was that if I failed at what I was trying to do, we might not be around much longer and that I would never have the chance to become a father. Missy finished talking, and then she told Kim that I wanted to say hello to her and handed me the phone.

"Hello, Kim, are you having fun with your aunt?" I asked.

"Hi, Michael. I know who you are now. I saw you on TV," Kim answered.

That was not exactly the reply I was expecting. Since I wasn't used to talking with kids, I didn't know enough about them to understand what they comprehended at certain ages.

Luckily for me, Kim kept the conversation going. "Aunt Ann says that you are a very good man and that you can talk to God."

Oh boy. Now I was really up shit's creek. *How the hell do I answer that?* I decided to take the easy way out. "Well, you can thank your aunt for saying that about me. I know your mom misses you and will see you soon. I have to go; it was great to talk to you. Bye," I said, ending the call and handing Missy back her phone.

The next two days were about the most enjoyable I had experienced in a very long time. Missy and I laughed, had pillow fights, and got to know each other better. She wasn't the same person I met the day I hurt my hand. She was funny, and her bright-green eyes seemed to sparkle even more.

I don't know what Rover did to her, but she seemed to make everything just a little bit brighter to me. She even tried to teach me to dance, though we didn't share the same taste in music and I would never be able to move the way she could. I decided to introduce her to the Grateful Dead, and by the time Friday morning came around, she was walking around singing "Sugar Magnolia" in a voice that I would have to say was absolutely amazing.

We did accomplish a few things of importance though. We found the right places to send the rest of the money, and I continued to bug Marty about getting the permit for the rally, which had yet to be approved. After we ate breakfast on Friday morning, I decided to call Marty once again.

"Good morning, Marty," I said when he answered his private line.

"Shit, Michael, what do want me to do? I have tried everything I can. I just don't think they want you to have this rally," Marty told me.

"What is their problem with me? It's not like I'm going to be preaching for people to overthrow the government. This is about encouraging people to try to be better humans for Christ sake," I said.

"Let's face facts, buddy, you are a polarizing figure, and a lot of people still wish you were dead. In their minds, a lot of people would like to make you that way permanently, which means the chances of violence erupting at this rally are pretty good. So that means lots of security would be needed, and that costs money, which they do not want to spend," Marty told me.

"Well, screw them, Marty. I don't care if I have to rent a semitruck and stand on top of it with a megaphone. I am announcing this rally tonight on Bob's show, and they are just going to have to deal with all of the people who are going to come out to be a part of it," I said.

"OK, I'll keep trying. Maybe they'll bend once they see the reaction people have to you after your appearance on the show," he said.

"Thanks, Marty," I answered.

"Michael, knock it out of the park tonight!" Marty said.

"I'll do my best," I said and ended the call.

I had heard the doorbell ring while I was on the phone with Marty, and I saw Nancy come in when Missy opened the door. She had brought the final batch of checks for me to sign.

"Hi, Nancy," I said, taking the envelope with the checks from her.

"I heard you talking to Marty, Michael. I can tell you he has done everything he could to get that permit pushed through. Believe me; I know," Nancy said.

"I know he did, Nancy. I'm not upset with him," I told her.

"Michael, everyone at the firm is rooting for you. Even some of the people that wouldn't say it out loud," she said.

"Thanks, Nancy. I'm going to need all the support I can get," I said smiling at her.

I opened the envelope and signed all of the checks and then handed them back to Nancy. Just as I did, the doorbell rang again. Missy opened the door. It was Steve. "Michael, we should get going now. I checked the traffic reports, and we might run into some construction delays on the way," he said. Missy gave Nancy a hug before she left, and I smiled and waved good-bye to her.

"All right, Steve. I'm ready when you are. Missy, are you all set?" I asked.

"I'm ready," Missy said grabbing her bag.

We followed Steve to the elevators and out the front of the building. There was a large black limo and a large black SUV waiting for us out on the street. All of Steve's guys were around the limo, looking in every direction for any signs of trouble.

The driver of the limo got out, but I didn't recognize him. "Michael, this is Charlie. He'll be driving the limo," Steve told me.

Charlie walked over to me and Missy and shook our hands.

"It is a pleasure to meet you, Mr. Ryan," Charlie said.

"Thank you; nice to meet you too, Charlie. This is Missy Franzone," I replied.

"I know who you are, Miss Franzone," Charlie said as he opened the door to the limo for us.

Missy and I got into the back, and Steve followed us. The men Steve had brought with him all got into the SUV parked behind the limo.

"Excuse me, Charlie, does this limo have privacy glass?" I asked.

"Yes, Mr. Ryan; it's the red button right above your head. The green button will lower the glass," Charlie answered.

"Thank you, please excuse us for a moment," I said.

I pushed the red button, and the tinted glass rose up and sealed us off from the driver. "OK, Steve, who is this guy and why is he here?" I asked.

"Michael, relax; this guy has driven dignitaries and CEOs, and he's skilled in evasive driving tactics. He is expertly trained to drive this limo, which, by the way, is bulletproof, meaning it is very heavy and not the easiest thing to handle when you need to make a quick getaway. Besides, we need every one of us available to try and keep you two safe. With Charlie driving, we can concentrate on just that," Steve told us.

I looked over at Missy. "He makes sense, Michael. This Charlie guy must know his stuff," she said.

"OK, well, let's get going," I said, reaching for the green button to lower the screen.

"One more thing, Michael," Steve said as my hand stopped before it reached the button. "Just in case you're wondering why I am the only one in the limo with you two, I saw the way some of the guys were looking at you, Ms. Franzone. I didn't want you to feel uncomfortable on our ride up," Steve said.

"Thank you very much," Missy said.

I lowered the screen, and Charlie turned and looked back at us. "Is everything OK, Mr. Ryan?" Charlie asked.

"Yes, Charlie, everything's fine; let's get on our way, and please call me Michael."

"Charlie, do you have some way to attach an iPod to the sound system?" Missy asked.

"Yes, under the audio controls, there is a compartment that opens; you'll find it in there," Charlie answered. Missy pulled my iPod out of her bag and plugged it in. It had nothing but Grateful dead music on it, and Steve seemed to like what he was hearing. I wasn't so sure about Charlie.

"Nice," Steve said.

"You like the Grateful Dead?" Missy asked.

"I'm from San Francisco, Missy," Steve answered thinking that Missy would know what that meant.

She looked over at me and gave me an inquisitive look. "The Grateful Dead are from the San Francisco area, Missy," I told her.

"I see," she said.

I sat back and started to think back on my life. I had a hard time remembering what it was like before this all began. I knew Zack had guided me to find him; he had even put the idea in my head for the story that would eventually lead me to him.

I still didn't understand why he chose me. I had learned from experience that Zack's words didn't always contain the whole message. He left clues to his meaning in his actions, as well. I decided to clear my mind, just listen to the music, and try to enjoy the ride. The song, "Going down the Road Feeling Bad," was playing. I smiled and closed my eyes.

The ride didn't seem that long to me as I suppose I lost myself in the music. The sound of my phone ringing brought me back to reality. It was Bob calling. "Hi, Bob," I said.

"Where are you?" Bob asked. I looked out the window of the limo.

"We are in the city, probably fifteen minutes from you," I answered guessing on the time thing.

"OK, we have a bit of a mob scene here, so let me call you back. The NYPD is here, and they have asked us to let them get this under control before you arrive," Bob said.

"All right, call me back when they are ready for us," I told him.

"What's wrong?" Missy asked.

"Charlie, how far are we from the studio?" I asked.

"Fifteen blocks," Charlie answered.

"It seems they are having a little problem with crowd management, and the police have been called in to get things under control. They've asked us to hold off on our arrival until things are a little calmer," I told them.

Steve grabbed his radio and told the men in the SUV behind us what was going on. "Michael, you're sure you want to go through with this?" Steve asked.

"Yes, Steve. I'm sure. I'm going on Bob's show tonight," I replied.

The limo jerked as Charlie must have slammed on the brakes.

"Charlie, what's wrong?" Steve asked.

"That!" Charlie said pointing toward the front of the limo. We all looked out the front windshield, and all we could see were two huge paws and legs. I reached for the door handle, but it was locked and none of the buttons I pressed on the door would release the lock.

"Charlie, unlock this thing," I said.

The driver just sat there.

"Charlie, I said to unlock this fucking thing now!" This time, I shouted at him. Charlie snapped out of his daze and unlocked the doors.

I stepped out of the limo, and Missy followed me. I knew better than to tell her to stay in the car. She wouldn't have listened to me if I had. I heard the doors of the SUV open, and I turned around and put my hand up in a gesture that told them to stay put. Steve was halfway in and out of the limo. I turned to look at him.

"You and your men stay in the vehicles," I told him. I looked up at Rover; he must have been at least thirty-five feet tall. "I guess you know about our little crowd problem," I said.

Rover nodded his head and then made a motion I interpreted as "follow me."

"All right, we're going to get back in the limo and tell the driver to follow you," I said.

Rover nodded and stood up. I might have been a little off on the height thing; he was huge. Missy grabbed my arm and dug her nails into my skin. "We're fine," I told her.

"Michael, look around us," Missy said.

I guess I had been too preoccupied to notice I didn't hear anyone else but us. This was New York City, and there was no noise—no sounds of people; it was eerie. Missy and I got back into the limo.

"Charlie, follow Rover," I said.

"Michael, there isn't any traffic in front of us or behind us. The cars, the trucks, the buses—they all just vanished," Charlie said. This seemed to freak everyone out, but I had seen Zack's power enough times that this did not faze me a bit.

"Everybody chill the fuck out. I need to call Bob and let him know we're coming," I said. I dialed Bob, and he answered on the first ring.

"Hey, it's still pretty chaotic over here. The suits are wondering if they should shut this thing down," Bob told me.

"I don't think that would be a very good idea, Bob. We're coming in with our own very large crowd controller," I said.

"Michael, what are you talking about? I'm telling you it is a mob scene out here," Bob replied.

"I'll see you in a few," I said, ending the call.

Every street we turned on was empty; there weren't any cars or people or anything on them. Rover suddenly stopped walking, and Charlie stopped the limo. "How close are we, Charlie?" I asked.

"We need to drive up one block and then a left, and we are there," Charlie answered.

"What are you thinking, Michael?" Missy asked.

"Look, I might be way off base on this, but I think Rover wants me to walk there with him. I think Zack wants to show everyone his power and that what I am saying and doing is what he wants," I said.

120

"All right then, we walk together hand in hand," Missy answered.

"OK, then let's do it," I said.

"Steve, you and your men can walk with us too if you want," I told him.

"Charlie, you follow us in the limo, and, Steve, make sure that the driver of the SUV stays behind the limo," I told them. I wanted to keep the vehicles close just in case.

Missy and I got out of the limo while Steve used his radio to tell the men behind us what we were doing. Rover turned his head back and watched us get out. Four of the men who came with Steve joined us. "OK, we're going to walk in front of Rover," I said.

"In front?" Steve asked.

"Yes, in front. I am not hiding from anyone," I answered.

Rover didn't move as we all positioned ourselves in front of him. "Let's go," I said, and I began to walk. Everyone followed my lead.

As big as Rover was, he needed to wait for us to walk a bit before he took a step or he would have crushed one of us with his paw. I could hear the sounds of people chanting as we got closer to the corner. It got louder with each step, and I was soon able to make out some of what they were screaming.

"Die, devil worshipper!" and "We will accept no false god!" were just some of the things I heard. I could also hear a police officer speaking through a megaphone telling them this was an unlawful demonstration and they must disperse. We were only about two hundred feet from the corner, and Steve and his men began to try to surround Missy and me.

"Steve, thank you. Protect Missy if you want, but I need the people to see me. Rover will not let anything happen to me, I assure you," I said.

121

Steve acknowledged that he understood, and he and his men moved away from me. Missy came right to my side. "We're in this together, remember?" she said to me as she grabbed my hand and squeezed it.

We came around the corner, and I could now see the huge crowd. Bob was right there too. There must have been a couple thousand people; they stretched as far as I could see down the street.

I saw a police officer standing on top of what looked like a UPS truck, but I think it was actually a prisoner transport truck. He was holding a microphone. It must have been him I heard trying to clear the area. He lifted the microphone to his mouth and began to speak just as Rover came into sight. "Holy fucking shit!" was all he was able to say when he saw Rover. After that, all I heard was screaming. I saw people dropping their signs and running. It took all of five minutes before there was nothing on the streets but dropped signs and empty police vehicles since all of them ran as well.

"You want to explain to me what just happened here?" Steve asked.

"I wish I could," I answered.

"Why did they all run, Michael? Even the police ran," Missy added.

"It looks like not everyone ran," I said pointing to the three people I saw standing behind one of the barriers the police had put up.

"Michael!" I heard a familiar voice call. It was Domenique Williams. She was standing with her parents, Melody and James. I started to walk toward them, and Domenique ran to me. When she reached me, she put her arms around my waist and hugged me tightly. "I'm so glad you aren't dead," she said to me.

"I'm pretty glad about that myself," I said, giving her a hug back. Domenique's mother, Melody, was the next one to greet me.

"Hello, Michael. It is so good to see you again," she said and kissed me on the cheek.

Her husband, James, was right behind her, and I reached out my hand to shake his. "Hello, James," I said. "I want all of you to meet Missy," I said. "Missy, this is—"

Missy stopped me before I could finish. "Melody and James Williams, and this must be Domenique," she said. She shook hands with Melody and James and turned to Domenique.

"Are you a movie star?" Domenique asked Missy.

"No, honey; I'm just a mom, and just like your mother, I have a daughter about your age," Missy answered her.

"You're really pretty," Domenique said.

"Thank you, Domenique," Missy replied.

"So, I assume this is Rover?" James asked.

"Yes, he keeps popping up, usually when we need him," I answered. I looked up at Rover. "I think we're OK now, Rover. Thank you for getting us here safely," I said.

Rover must have agreed that we were safe because he transformed himself back to normal size. I think everyone felt more at ease with him being that way.

Rover then walked over to Domenique and licked her face. I had never seen him show any sign off normal dog-type behavior before, but it was a nice thing to see. Domenique laughed and gave Rover a hug around his neck. "Where is he, Michael? Where is Zack?" she asked.

"I don't know, Domenique, but I'm sure he'll show himself when he thinks the time is right. I'm pretty confident you will see him again very soon."

"Now that is a fucking entrance," I heard Bob's voice behind me. I turned around and saw him coming out of the front door of the building.

Like me, Bob had never had children, but unlike me, he had never learned how to behave when he was around them.

"Hi, Bob," I said walking over to shake his hand.

"Damn, you really do look thirty years younger, and who is that babe over there? Jesus, she is smoking hot!"

"That is Missy. Would you like to meet her?" I asked.

"What do you think?" Bob replied, and he walked over to Missy. "Bob Matlin, and it is a pleasure to meet you, Missy," Bob said using all the charm he could muster up.

"Nice to meet you too, and please give it a rest," Missy replied, letting him know his charm would get him nowhere with her.

I walked over to Bob and touched him on the shoulder to get his attention. "Have you looked around? There aren't any people on the streets, and other than the vehicles that were left here when everyone ran, there are no cars. Listen, do you hear any noises? Do you hear anything other than us?" I asked.

Bob's eyes opened wide, and he turned his head to look in every direction. "Holy shit, you're right! There's nothing. No sounds, no cars, no people. How can that be?"

"All right, we're going to go inside, and I am hoping that Rover will bring all the people and the other stuff back once he knows that no harm will come to us," I said. I had no fucking idea whether that would actually happen or what Rover had done with all the people, but I didn't have a whole lot of options at the moment. "Bob, is there a side entrance out of here?" I asked.

"Yeah, there is a service entrance down the alley," Bob said pointing to where the alley was.

"Steve, I think we should pull the cars back there," I said. He nodded in agreement. "Also, please make sure that Missy and the Williams are kept safe. I think you can see that I'll be fine," I added.

"You got it, Michael," Steve said, and he walked over to tell the men with him what they should do.

Chapter Nine

As Bob led us into the building, he was having a very hard time tearing his eyes away from Missy. "You know, she's going knock you on your ass if you don't stop staring at her," I whispered to Bob.

He smiled. "Sorry, but she is just amazing," he replied.

Bob walked over to the security desk, stopped, and turned around. "Is he coming with us?" he asked, pointing to Rover, who was standing at my side.

"I don't know. He doesn't take his orders from me, Bob," I answered.

"Well, this may be crazy, but I'm told you understand English so I'm going to talk directly to you," Bob said looking at Rover.

"Go on; he understands every word you say," I said.

"If you come up with us, the other guests might be too scared to talk. Maybe even too scared to come on the show. I was hoping you might consider staying down here in the lobby; I assure you Michael is safe in the studio," Bob asked still looking right at Rover.

Rover turned and looked at me. "I think he might be right, Rover, and I think we're pretty safe up there, but thank you for getting us here," I said.

Rover turned and started walking toward the front door, but after a few steps, he simply vanished. "Wow, now that's something you don't see every day," Bob said.

"Bob, I'd like you to meet Melody, James, and Domenique Williams," I said.

"I just read *Mr. Breeze* again, Michael. I know who the Williams are. It is a pleasure to meet you," Bob said.

"Thank you, Mr. Matlin. Melody and I love your show," James said.

"Thank you, and please call me Bob," Bob said shaking their hands.

Bob signed us all in at the front desk, and we took the elevator up to the sixteenth floor. The doors opened, and we saw people walking back and forth in every direction.

A man with a clipboard came up to Bob as soon as we exited the elevator. "Bob, we're going to be doing sound checks in about fifteen minutes," he said.

"Dave, stop for a second," Bob said. The man stopped walking and turned around to face us. "Michael, this Dave Rubick, my producer," Bob said.

"Nice to meet you, Dave," I said, and I reached out my hand to him.

"Same here, Michael, but please excuse me; we still have a lot to get done before we go on the air," Dave said, and he walked away before I had the chance to introduce anyone else.

"What's up? Why is everyone so rushed?" I asked.

"This is not our normal studio, Michael. They do the news here. The network is borrowing this place because we are not using an audience, and they thought they could keep the place we were shooting a secret," Bob told us.

"I guess that plan didn't work out so well," I replied.

"Nope, not at all, and they have to redo the set and get things ready for us. We go on in a little over an hour," Bob said. "Well, let's get all of you settled. Follow me," Bob told us. He pointed to an empty dressing room. "You and your family can watch everything from in here," he told James.

"Thanks. And, Michael, good luck," James said as he walked Domenique into the room.

"Go get 'em, Michael," Melody said. I just smiled at them.

Bob walked us a little further down the hall to the door that had a piece of paper with my name taped on it. "Nice touch," I said opening the door and letting Missy enter first.

Bob closed the door once we were all inside the room. "So, who else did you get to come on the show with me?" I asked.

Bob always started his show talking to whomever his special guest was, and for the last half hour, he had three or four guests engage in a panel-type debate—or screaming match, depending upon the civility of his guests.

"Well, we asked the pharmaceutical industry to send a spokesman, and they said, 'No, thanks.' We also asked pretty much every mainstream religious group to send someone, and they all declined. Then we called every politician I have ever had on the show, and they all said no, as well," Bob said.

"OK, I guess that makes sense. So, who did say yes?" I asked.

"Do you remember the group that was going around to schools demanding they burn all the books that taught about evolution?" Bob asked.

"I remember; they were on the news a lot over the last year," Missy said.

"We have the leader of that group, Ann Hawks," Bob said.

"So who is on the other side of that issue?" I asked knowing that if Bob had a fundamentalist on there, he would need someone with the exact opposite view.

"We have Dr. Adrienne Franklin with us," Bob told us.

"Who is Dr. Franklin?" Missy asked.

"Dr. Adrienne Franklin is what they call a Darwinist. She believes there was no God, no Adam and Eve, and that we evolved from Apes. I spoke with her once, years ago, when I was researching a story," I answered.

"Yeah, she remembers you, Michael. She seemed to think you were in agreement with her on this stuff," Bob said.

"Well, back then, she was probably right about that," I said.

"And who else agreed to come on tonight?" I asked, knowing that there would be one other member on tonight's panel. "We have ex-congressman, Max Barker, who is now an ordained minister, with us," Bob answered.

"You're fucking kidding me, right?" I asked.

"I told you we had a hard time finding anyone to come on with you," Bob said.

I saw that Missy didn't know who Max Barker was, so I decided to fill her in.

"Max Barker was a congressman for one term in South Carolina, and there was, or maybe still is, a law on the books there that prohibits anyone under eighteen from playing pinball machines. Max thought it was such a good idea that the whole nation should adopt it and it should come with a prison term for anyone who lets underage users play the machines. If I remember correctly, he ended up resigning before his first year was up," I said.

"Yeah, he never made it through the first year," Bob confirmed.

"Listen, I'm not going to do my usual monologue tonight. I'm going to introduce you, and then we will talk for about fifteen minutes and then bring the other three on with us. I have to run a sound check and makeup— you know the drill. See you out there," Bob said, and then he left the room. "So, it sounds like this is going to be quite a circus," Missy said.

"This is television, Missy. They have to make it entertaining, so I'm not surprised," I said.

"This isn't on regular TV, right? So people need to subscribe to a pay service to see this show?" she asked.

"Yes, and I think I see where you're going with this. I'm counting on word of mouth and other media to spread the word about what I say tonight. I'm also hoping that the news about the rally ends up on the front page of most newspapers across the country," I said. Missy nodded and gave me one of those "good thinking" looks. "Let's go see the Williams. I need to tell them what's going on. We do have a few extra rooms on that floor we rented at the hotel, right?" I asked.

"Yes, we do," Missy answered.

The door was open, and they were all eating when we walked in. "I'm glad they brought you all something to eat," I said.

"They're being very nice to us, Michael," Melody said.

"Look, I'm long since past questioning Zack's methods or motives for what he does. Whatever Rover did to scare everyone away earlier did

131

involve the three of you, which tells me you're supposed to be here, and I think you're supposed to come back to DC with us. You see, I'm only going on this show to announce that I plan on having a rally on the National Mall next Wednesday—a rally for peace and equality for everyone all over the world. I'm going to ask people not only in our country to come, but for others all over the world to gather together at the same time, for the same cause," I said.

James stood up and walked over to me; he reached out his hand to me. "Michael, you're asking a black family to join you in a rally for equality. What do you think our answer is going to be?" James said smiling as we shook hands.

"Thanks, James, I think we both know what Zack is capable of. I just hope we can bring out enough people to make him see that we can change and that we just need more time to get there," I said. "OK, you all enjoy the show. We'll come get you when it's over, and we'll all head back to DC," I said as Missy and I left the room.

There was a tray of sandwiches and various drinks waiting for us when we got back to my dressing room. The makeup person was also there waiting for me. Once the makeup was done, a young woman came into the room. She stopped dead in her tracks when she saw Missy, giving her that look women sometimes give when they see a woman who is so much more attractive than they are.

"You are on in fifteen minutes, Mr. Ryan. Someone will be back to take you to the studio," she said turning and leaving the room. "What the fuck was that about? Did I steal her boyfriend in a previous life?" Missy exclaimed.

"No. Someone once told me that men are jealous of other men for what they have and women are jealous of other women for the way they look. I have found over the years that tends to be true for most people," I said.

Missy smiled and started to chuckle. "You know, there might just be something to that," she said.

The fifteen minutes seemed to go by in record time, and I was brought into the studio and asked to sit on the end of an L-shaped table. There was one chair next to the one I was sitting in, which I assumed was Bob's, and three more on the long side, which should be for the other three guests. They had agreed to let Missy sit in the control room, and from where I sat, I could see her.

Bob came into the studio dressed impeccably in an expensive and perfectly tailored suit, shirt, and tie. His hair looked as if it were a piece of sculpture rather than hair; it was so perfect, not a strand out of place. "Are you ready for this?" Bob asked me.

"Let's do it," I replied. I saw Dave, Bob's producer, coming toward me.

"Michael, we're going to dim the lights back here and just shine them on Bob for the opening of the show. Then, we'll light up the whole area when Bob sits down with you," Dave said.

"Got it," I answered.

The lights dimmed, and I sat and waited. I read the countdown from five, and then the lights came on and focused on Bob standing in the center of the studio.

"Good evening, and welcome to a very special airing of *Pass the Buck*. We have a lot of firsts here tonight, one being that I am not going to do my usual monologue. Second, we are coming to you live for the very first time and are filming this without a studio audience. The reason that we have no audience tonight is because of my special guest, Michael Ryan.

"First of all, let me say this. I have known Michael Ryan for over fifteen years, and I have never known him to use any story for his own personal gain. The man I know is no saint, but he is certainly not a pawn of the devil as some of you with the brain power of a flea have accused him of being. Michael Ryan has come here tonight to talk about *Mr. Breeze* and the reason he decided to come out of hiding."

Since there was no live audience, there wasn't any applause or any booing. Bob just turned and walked over to the L-shaped table and sat down in the empty chair next to me.

"I want to thank you for the courage you have shown over the years, not only with writing *Mr. Breeze*, but for all the stories you have written. I know your life has been threatened many times over the years, and I thank you for being here tonight," he said.

"Thanks, Bob."

"So, how does a guy who spent years writing about corruption in government, hate groups, wars, and selling people into servitude end up writing *Mr. Breeze*? And you made how much money on that book?"

"It really is just like it was written in *Mr. Breeze*. At the time, I thought it was my own idea to write something about good things that were happening in the world. But, as it turned out, Zack had put those thoughts into my head. He wanted me to write this story, and I wrote it exactly as it happened. I did make well over a billion dollars from the sales of *Mr. Breeze*, but over the last week, I have donated all of that money to various charities," I answered.

"You gave away more than a billion dollars in a week, and you did not call me? I thought we were friends!"

I smiled. I knew Bob would be adding some humor in when he could.

"Well, Bob, last time I checked, you were not exactly a charity case."

Bob smiled. I think he realized I was able to throw in my own bits of humor.

"So you call me and say, 'Hey, Bob, I'm alive,' and tell me you want to be on my show and you want it to be tonight. What gives?"

"You're right. I have never been what you'd call a saint and, like you, have never had any use for religion of any kind. But for some reason, I still don't know why Zack chose me to write *Mr. Breeze*. I hope that all of you out there have read *Mr. Breeze*, and if you haven't, you need to now, because we all have to understand that Zack has the power to do what he has said and our survival depends on us all listening to his words."

"For those who have not read *Mr. Breeze*, what do we need to do?"

"Well, for one thing, we need to stop letting our egos control us. We are not the most powerful beings on this planet. Our armies and our weapons are useless against a being like Zack. He showed us kindness by curing our diseases, and when the drug companies realized their survival was at stake, they convinced us the cures were only temporary, and we were so stupid we believed it. Let me ask you this; has anyone died of cancer in the last two years? Has anyone contracted any of the many diseases that we didn't have a cure for in the last two years? Bob, when you told me that no one from the pharmaceutical industry would appear on this show with me, I wasn't surprised. Why would they? They lied to everyone to make a profit. Was I surprised that no one from any mainstream religious group would come on this show with me? No, I was not. After all, how would any of them have been able to justify the things that were done and said? Zack told me that money would end up being our downfall and that fear has always been used by some to control others. Religion has been used for thousands of years to control the masses. In earlier times, many feared the gods, and in more modern times, we have used religion as a weapon in politics and as a basis for war and hatred. They want to call Zack the devil because he wants us to live in peace and to respect each other. Let me ask all of you in the FAD what you would call yourselves since you seem to preach just the opposite? I came here tonight, not to defend Zack or even myself. I came here to ask all of you to help me show Zack we are worthy of existence and to announce that I intend to have a rally next Wednesday on the National Mall at noon. I ask everyone everywhere to join me, whether it be at the Mall or a place you gather in your own country or your own state or town. If you believe in peace, if you believe in equality for all, you have an open invitation to join me. But if you believe in hatred, in separation, whether it be for color, race, gender, or religion, then I ask you to stay away."

"Michael, do you really think we are in danger from this Zack person?"

"Come on now, Bob, after everything I just said, you ask me if Zack poses a threat to us? You told me you just read *Mr. Breeze* again, and, if you did, you would know what I know. For those of you who have not read it or don't remember it, just read the last page. That should give you what you need to know. As for what I think, I believe he is disgusted with us, but to call him a threat to mankind, that is a bit of a stretch, since without him, I do not believe there would be a mankind."

"So, what should all of us do? Pray? Give away all our money like you did? Tell us what to do, Michael."

"Trust me, Bob, if I knew what would make a total difference, I would tell you. And I am not here to say the world is coming to an end. You see, I'm winging this, but someone needs to try something, and if no one else will, then I guess that someone has to be me. I am in no position to make judgments, only observations. And from what I see, our great society is not so great at all."

"Well, I cannot argue with you there, and if you could put in a word to Zack and ask him to wipe out every reality TV star, in my opinion, that would be a giant step in the right direction. OK, seriously, why you? Why did this Zack choose you? What's so special about Michael Ryan? I mean look at you, you're—what?—fifty-four, fifty-five, and you suddenly look thirty, and your body looks like you spend every waking hour in the gym. Why Michael Ryan?"

I smiled. I knew Bob would keep trying to throw some humor in the show.

"I cannot answer that question, Bob. I haven't spoken to or seen Zack since the day I was shot. I don't know why I have been changed physically, but it does feel great to be young again."

"So this rally is your idea; this Zack person didn't tell you to do this?" he asked.

"No, he did not tell me to do it, and since I'm sure you're going to ask, he also didn't tell me to give away all the money I made from sales of *Mr. Breeze*, either."

"I have to ask you one more question before we bring our panel out. What about people like the FAD and whoever fire-bombed your house and tried to kill you? What would you say to them? Surely you must be angry at those people for what they preach and what they have done."

I saw the three chairs on the other side of the table being filled. The guests were all being fitted with microphones, so I knew the real fun was about to begin.

"Yes, I was very angry about everything that happened in the six months before my house was destroyed. I was angry, but now my anger has been replaced with purpose. The only thing I can say to those who wished me harm is, why? All I did was write a story. If you remember from reading the book, if I didn't write that story, we wouldn't be here right now. I am here to ask everyone to put aside their hate and to realize that Zack's warning is for all of us. He does not distinguish between you and the people you choose to hate, and, as much as any of you may think you are in the right, I can assure you he does not care about your cause; nor is it of any relevance to him. So I say this to all of you out there who preach hate: it's over. You need to face the fact that our maker does not differentiate. We either learn to live together, or we will perish together."

"Strong words, Michael, and now I want to bring on our panel. First, we have Dr. Adrienne Franklin. Dr. Franklin is a Harvard professor and the author of the book, *There Is No God*. She is the face of the world's Darwinist movement. Next, here is Ms. Ann Hawks. Ms. Hawks is the leader of the fundamentalist group, Save Our Families. And finally, the former congressman and, now, an ordained minister of the Church of the Higher Path, Max Barker. I want to thank all of you for being here tonight, and I would like to start with you, Dr. Franklin. What do you make of all this, and who do you think this Zack person is?"

"I want to thank you for having me here tonight, Bob, and I must say I do agree with Mr. Ryan on a few points. Our society is a mess, and we have allowed religions to control far too many people's thoughts for much too long. I also think that the being he calls Zack did cure all of our diseases and the pharmaceutical industry used fear in the same way that religious groups did to get people to come back to them. What I cannot agree on is that this Zack is our God or that he is even a human being. I would suggest he come forward and allow us to examine him so we can determine what he really is," Dr. Franklin said.

"So, you want to ask God to take a physical?"

"That is ridiculous, Bob! We are all aware of Dr. Franklin's views. I believe she will be arguing heaven's existence even as she stands at the pearly gates. I read your little book, Mr. Ryan, and it touched me deeply, and I, too, believe as your friend Zack said, that our modern world has made us grow farther apart even though our technological advances allow us to communicate faster and easier. What I don't understand is why you, Mr. Ryan? Why were you chosen to write this book, and why does this Zack choose to communicate to you, a nonbeliever by your own admission? I will come to your rally, though, and I hope everyone from Save Our Families will also support your rally, because I believe in what you are doing. If this Zack being is our God, then I hope he will shine his light down on all of us that day."

I did not believe in anything this woman's group stood for, but it wasn't my place to judge and if I was going to make this work, I was going to have to put my own prejudices aside and welcome anyone who was willing to participate.

"Thank you, Ms. Hawks," I said. "You and your group are more than welcome to join us."

"You are a charlatan and a pawn of the devil, Michael Ryan," Max Barker interjected. "You think we didn't see how you arrived today with the devil dog leading you and your little group? I saw that beast and what he did to the crowd outside this building. A crowd of decent Americans who wanted to take a stand against evil. I speak to God every day, Mr. Ryan, and that abomination you call Zack is not the God that speaks to me or the God I worship. This rally of yours is nothing but the devil's recruiting station."

Well, I now knew how the news of where we were filming leaked out. Max Barker had told them. He was like a dog with a bone, and he was not going to let go of this. I considered him a lost cause.

Bob broke in. "So, Max, you say you speak to God and he speaks to you. Tell me, what exactly does he say?"

"Congressman Barker," Dr. Franklin said, "you must realize that what you're saying makes no sense and has no basis in fact. You claim you can have conversations with God. I find that statement completely ridiculous."

"Well then, you must be in with the devil as well, Dr. Franklin," Max concluded.

Bob started to laugh, clearly pleased with the interactions his guests were having.

"Michael, what do you have to say in your defense?" he said.

"Bob, first of all, I am not here to defend myself, and I am certainly not here to defend Zack, as he is more than capable of doing that himself. There are five of us sitting here, all with different views of God, religion, and how we should live our lives, but all five of us and everyone out there who is watching this needs to understand that Zack does not care about any of that and neither should you. Dr. Franklin does not believe in anything that can't be proven scientifically, and I can understand that since I once felt somewhat the same. Ms. Hawks, you believe that God is responsible for everything, no matter how much evidence there is to the contrary. And you, Congressman, I don't know what you believe in, though it seems you are more interested in stirring up controversy and publicity than preaching what you call 'God's word.' You all have a right to believe in what you want, just like everyone who is watching this does. Me, I believe in none of it. I now know that in order to survive, we need to believe in ourselves. Yes, Ms. Hawks, and yes, Congressman Barker, Zack chose me, and I watched what he did and felt his power, or divinity, if that works better for you, just being in his presence. He is our maker, whether you like it or not, and he can choose to follow through with what he promised. All of you can sit here and make whatever arguments you like, but in the end, like I said earlier, we are all in this together, so once again, I ask all of you to help me save all of humanity."

There was silence after I finished speaking. I was not sure whether my words moved them or they were just surprised by them.

Dr. Franklin spoke first. "You make an interesting argument, Mr. Ryan, but scientists need proof. Without proof, science isn't fact; it is just science fiction."

"Do you need proof to believe in yourself, Dr. Franklin? Because, essentially, that is all I am asking."

Dr. Franklin smiled. "No, Mr. Ryan, I do not."

"This is blasphemy!" Barker railed. "You are all being hypnotized by this man. The devil has many faces and will use anyone or anything to take your soul. I will not sit here and be a part of this any longer. I ask all of you God-fearing people to rise up and fight the devil and his minions, wherever they are."

Once Max Barker finished speaking, he pulled off his microphone and walked off the set.

"And I am taking my ball and going home since you won't play by my rules." Bob spoke in a childish tone, clearly mocking Max's outburst and his leaving the stage.

Ann said, "What do you want from us. How can we help?"

"Michael, has Zack asked you to do this?" Bob asked.

"Those are pretty good questions. I will answer the easy one first. No, Zack has not asked me to do this. This is all my idea. How can you help?

Well, for a start, by doing what I did not too long ago. Look inside yourself and ask if you are the best person you can be. Can you be more giving, more understanding, and more tolerant? Can you stop looking at what makes us different and start looking at what makes us all the same?"

Dr. Franklin said, "I must say, Mr. Ryan, I had my doubts about you, and I was wary about being associated with what might be discussed on this program, but I am now glad that I came on with you. I still don't believe your assertions about this Zack, but I do believe you are genuinely trying to help make the world a better place for everyone, and, for that, I commend you."

"Well, that is all we have time for tonight. I would like to thank my guests: Ann Hawks, Dr. Alan Franklin, the now departed Max Barker, and a special thanks to Michael Ryan."

Both Ann Hawks and Dr. Franklin came over, shook my hand, and wished me luck before they left the studio. I saw Missy coming toward me. She was smiling.

"That was amazing! I have never been so proud of anyone in my life," she said, and then she gave me a hug.

"My name is Bob Matlin. It is very nice to meet you," Bob said jokily as he reached out his hand toward me.

"Very funny," I said.

"I don't get the joke," Missy said.

"Well, I have known Michael a long time, and the guy who was here tonight was not the guy I used to know. That guy only cared about one thing—getting the story," Bob said.

"People change, Bob. Sometimes by choice, other times by necessity," I said.

141

"Well, it was a great show, Michael. Thank you for doing this," Bob said, and he turned to walk away.

"We have a slight problem, people," Dave Rubick said.

Bob stopped and turned around. "What's the problem?" he asked.

"I can't explain this, but we are on every channel, and it appears we are being televised everywhere," Dave said.

"What? How is that possible. Can't you cut the feed?" Bob said.

"We cut the feed ten minutes ago; in fact, we even cut the power after you were done. It made no difference," Dave said.

"When you say everywhere, what exactly does that mean?" I asked.

"What it means is that the live show we just did is being shown on every channel of every television, and from what I can see so far, in every country and in all languages," Dave answered.

"So, if someone in France turns on their television, they see the show, but they hear it in French?" Missy asked.

"Yes, and that is the only thing they can see because there is nothing else on anywhere, on any channel," Dave answered.

"Well, Michael, it looks like I am going international. Thanks, pal," Bob said half joking.

"What is it, Michael? Why are you smiling?" Missy asked. It just dawned on me, once again, Zack was using me or guiding me to suit his purpose.

"I have a feeling that this is the only thing anyone is going to be seeing on TV for a while," I said. I looked over and saw the Williams standing where we had filmed, and I waved them over. "I think it's time for us to go," I said. I shook hands again with Bob and with Dave, as well, and we made our way to the elevator and down to the lobby.

Steve and his men were waiting for us when the elevator doors opened. "Nice job, Michael," Steve said.

"Thanks, Steve. James, Melody, and Domenique are coming in the limo with us. They will be staying at the hotel with you and your men. Please make sure they are kept safe," I said.

"Got it, and you two?" Steve asked.

"We'll be fine," I said.

"One thing you should know is that we have been monitoring the Internet, and the hate messages are increasing. There are videos of your house burning with messages like 'We should have made sure we got him last time' scrolling across the screen," Steve said.

"I guess you can't please everyone," I said half-jokingly.

"The dog has been outside the whole time, and we haven't seen anyone on the streets," Steve said.

"All right, then, let's get out of here," I said.

When I got outside, Rover looked over and I swear he grinned at me. The Williams got into the limo with us, and I sat back and got ready for the long ride home.

"What the fuck?" I heard Charlie say.

"Geez, Charlie, come on; there is a little girl back here," I told him.

Then I looked out the window of the limo. We were instantly back in Maryland, parked in front of the condo building. I reached around and patted

Charlie on the shoulder. "It's all right; I've seen this stuff before, and you never quite get used to it," I told him. "James and Melody, Steve and his men will take care of you. There are rooms waiting for you. I will be in touch tomorrow. Maybe Domenique would like to see some of the sights around DC. No one knows who you are, and you have nothing to be fearful of," I told them.

"Michael, what I saw you do tonight was perhaps the bravest and most unselfish thing I have ever witnessed. I am proud to know you. Whatever we can do to help you, just ask, and we will do it," James said.

"Michael, we just lost the Internet," Steve said.

"What do you mean, lost the Internet?" I asked.

"There is no signal. It's as if it's not out there," Steve replied.

We all picked up our phones.

"I have no signal either," Missy said.

"Me either," Melody chimed in.

I, too, was unable to access anything online.

"Well, maybe it's just a service glitch. I'm sure they'll fix it soon." I said. Missy and I said our good-byes and got out of the limo.

Steve followed us to the door. "Are you sure you're going to be OK by yourselves? That was some pretty bad shit they were putting online. They want you dead, Michael," Steve said.

"I know, Steve, but we'll be fine; I am certain of that," I told him.

Missy and I walked inside, and she looked over at me. "You're sure we're OK, right?" she asked.

"Yes, I am," I assured her.

Chapter Ten

O nce we were back in the condo, Missy tried to call her daughter. "Michael, I cannot get through on my cell phone. I'm getting the 'all networks are busy' message," she said.

"Try the landline in the kitchen," I said.

"It says, 'All circuits are busy; please try your call again later,'" she said.

I grabbed the laptop and tried, once again, to get online, but nothing happened. "I don't think this is a glitch. I think the Internet is gone," I said.

"Gone? How can it be gone?" Missy asked.

"How many times did you read *Mr. Breeze*, Missy? You know what Zack said about what would happen to our technology," I said. I could see Missy was searching her memory trying to remember Zack's words.

"But why wouldn't he start with our weapons?" she asked.

"I think he did," I answered.

"How, exactly, are we planning to hold this rally if the National Park Service doesn't issue the permit we need?" Missy asked.

"I have been thinking about that, and I think we should go down to the Park Service Monday morning and see if we can convince them to get off their butts and issue the permit," I answered.

Missy laughed. "You really think that's going to work?" she asked in a sarcastic tone.

"Well, if you have a better idea, I'm open to suggestions," I said in the same tone.

Missy smiled.

"I'm beat, and I think I'm going to call this an early night," I said.

"I'm going to stay up awhile and continue to try to reach Kim," Missy said.

"OK, good luck. Good night," I said.

"Michael, whatever happens after this, I just want you to know that I am grateful for you letting me be a part of this, and I think that what you are trying to do is truly remarkable," Missy said.

I smiled at her. "Thanks. I just hope it all works out," I said heading into my bedroom.

I fell asleep very quickly and was awakened the next morning when Missy sat on my bed, holding a newspaper. "Have a look. You made the front page. I love this headline, 'Michael Ryan speaks again and again and again,'" Missy said. "You were right about the Internet too," she added.

"What do you mean?" I asked as my head began to clear.

"Look on the column on the top right. 'Experts are baffled as the Internet goes down,'" Missy said.

I sat up in my bed and reached out my hand. Missy handed me the newspaper. Funny thing was, before Zack changed me, I would have needed reading glasses to read this, and my first reaction was still to look for them.

According to the articles, Bob's show was being played in a constant loop, and it was on every station in every country and was translated into whatever language was relevant. What really concerned me was the story about the Internet and that I was right. It was gone everywhere, and no one could explain how, or why, this had happened.

"Were you able to reach Kim last night?" I asked.

"Yes, it took a while, but I was able to get through on my cell phone," Missy answered.

"Everything OK?" I asked.

"Yes. Come on; get out of bed, and get dressed. We need to figure out how to make this rally happen. We need two plans: one for if we get the permit and a second one for if we do not," she said. Missy's enthusiasm was nice, but I was still trying to wake up completely.

"OK, give me a few minutes. I need to get myself together," I said.

Missy just sat there on the bed. "Missy, I need to go to the bathroom and put some clothes on," I said.

Missy chuckled, realizing I was naked. "OK, I'm outta here," she said. She left the bedroom, closing the door on her way out.

We spent most of the weekend coming up with plans for the rally, and we would occasionally turn the TV on to see if anything other than Bob's show was on. Nothing changed until eight o'clock Saturday night when the replays stopped and the TV went back to normal programming.

We watched as the news reports came in. First, they talked about what had happened with the normal programming. They said that the cause was under investigation and that the stations were in no way supporting any of the opinions that the guests of *Pass the Buck* had put forth.

It seemed the biggest story was the loss of the Internet though, and every station focused on it. It was such a huge story that all the major stations kept their news shows on right through the night. It reminded me of the way they covered big snowstorms, which I always thought was overkill.

Missy and I watched as they brought in expert after expert. Each one said something about not knowing what could have really caused the outage. This went on for the next twenty-four hours, and then finally, on Sunday night, they began to talk about the effects this would have on the stock exchanges opening the next morning.

Not only did the exchanges rely on the Internet, but a great many of the largest companies in the world required it to make money. Without it, there would be no search firms, no social networks, no online retailers. Many of these companies would now be worthless and out of business.

The bizarre thing about all of this was that not one person thought that there might be a connection to the fact that Bob's show was on for twenty-four hours straight, on every TV, in every language, and in every country in the world. No one commented about what Zack had said in *Mr. Breeze*— that our technology would be destroyed. I was astounded by the fact that we were really so arrogant that we refused to believe that we might not be in control of everything that was happening around us.

Missy and I went to bed early Sunday night. We had a lot of work to do the next day, and I had a feeling that it would take a while at the Park Service. I didn't, for a second, think they were just going to hand over the permit because we walked in the door.

I woke up early the next morning, made some coffee, and turned on the television. The number-one story was still the loss of the Internet. The stock markets would follow what the overseas markets had done and shut down today. I heard the front door open.

"Good morning," Missy said, walking into the living room wearing one of her rather revealing workout outfits. "Anything new?" she asked.

"Well, the Internet is still down, and the stock markets will not open today," I replied.

"Is there a rule about the markets closing for more than one day?" Missy asked.

"I think there might be, but I don't think they want a panic on their hands," I said.

"Meaning?" Missy asked.

"Well, let's say there is no more Internet. What happens to the value of a company like Google? It was worth billions on Friday; what would it be worth today?" I said.

"Oh shit, that would cause a panic, and it wouldn't be just Google that was worthless," Missy said. "The Internet is not coming back, is it, Michael?" she asked.

"I don't know, Missy. I just don't know," I answered.

"I'm going to shower and change. What time do you think the Park Service opens?" Missy asked.

Any other time, I would have just looked it up online, but not this time. "I assume they open at nine," I answered. I got off the couch and went in to shower, shave, and get dressed.

By the time we were finished, it was just about fifteen minutes to nine.

"I think I should give Marty a call before we go over there. Maybe he can give us the name of someone to talk to," I said.

"Good idea," Missy said.

As I hit the button to dial Marty's number, I heard the doorbell ring.

"I'll get it," Missy said.

"Make sure you check to see who it is first," I told her.

Missy looked through the peephole in the door and then over at me. "Put the phone down, Michael," she said as she opened the door.

"Good Morning, Ms. Franzone," Marty said as he walked into the condo.

"Marty, I was just calling you. What are you doing here?" I asked.

"Michael, there are six Secret Service agents downstairs in the lobby. They are here to bring you to the White House to see the president," Marty said.

"Why are you here, Marty?" I asked.

"After what happened in New York, they felt you would be less threatened if someone you knew came here to ask you to attend this meeting," Marty said.

"Really, in other words, they are afraid Rover might see them as a threat," I said. "All right, Marty, I'll go with them, but I would like Missy to come, as well," I said.

"I'm sorry, Michael, but I was told specifically that this meeting is with you and you alone," Marty said.

"It's all right, Michael; I'll be fine. You go," Missy said.

"Two Secret Service agents will stay in here and make sure Ms. Franzone is OK," Marty said.

"Well then, let's go. I'll see you in a little while," I said.

"Good luck," Missy said, as Marty and I walked out the front door.

Once we were in the elevator, I looked over at Marty. "Do you know what this is all about?" I asked.

"They didn't tell me anything, Michael. In fact, I was instructed not to mention any of this to anyone, ever," Marty said.

The elevator doors opened, and six men in dark suits were there waiting for us. "Mr. Ryan, I am Agent Garcia. If you don't mind, we will need to search you before we allow you to get into the car. Do you consent to this?"

"Yes, I do consent," I said and raised my arms. Agent Garcia was a well-built man; I guessed him to be in his early thirties. They checked me over by patting me down, as well as putting me through two different electronic screenings. I think they may have been looking to see if I had any recording devices on me, rather than any weapons.

"Michael, I have done what was asked of me, so I am going to head back downtown. Behave yourself," Marty said as he walked past me and out onto the street. Once they were satisfied I didn't have anything they did not want me to have, I was led outside. There was a large black sedan with all of its windows tinted so dark you couldn't see inside it. One of the agents opened the rear door for me, and I got in the backseat. Two of them, including Agent Garcia, got in the front seat and two others got into the car parked behind us. As Marty had said, two agents remained in the lobby of the condo to make sure Missy would be safe.

It wasn't a long ride from the condo to the White House, but neither agent spoke a word the entire time. It was strangely humorous to me that this was the first time I had been invited to the White House. I was not even acknowledged by the president after *Mr. Breeze* came out, and I knew they were well aware that my writing it had given all of mankind a second chance. I wasn't looking for a parade or even a medal back then, but a call or a thank-you note would have been a nice gesture.

When we got to the front gates, Agent Garcia reached over and handed one of the guards a piece of paper. After looking at it, the guard quickly opened the gates and waved us through. We drove around to the side of the building and stopped. Agent Garcia got out first and came around to open the car door for me.

"Follow me please, Mr. Ryan," he asked, and we walked up a few steps and through the doors that brought me into the West Wing of the White House. As Agent Garcia led me through the building, I was surprised by the fact that we were the only people there. It was Monday morning; this place should have been bustling with activity, and with the Internet crisis going on, it should even have been busier than normal.

Agent Garcia brought me to the doors of the Oval Office. The desks outside the office were empty. Not even the president's secretaries were there. "Go right in, Mr. Ryan; he is expecting you," Agent Garcia told me.

I opened the door, walked in, and closed it behind me. The president was sitting behind his desk but got up as soon as he saw me. "It is very nice to finally meet you, Mr. Ryan," the president said, shaking my hand.

"Thank you, Mr. President. The pleasure is all mine," I replied.

"Please sit down," he said, motioning to two chairs in the middle of the Oval Office. There was a table between the chairs and a copy of *Mr. Breeze*, which was full of bookmarks, on it.

"First of all, Mr. Ryan, the conversation we are about to have never happened. You are not here, and you and I have never met. Do you understand?" the president commanded.

Well, now I knew why there was no one there. "Yes, sir, Mr. President; I understand," I replied.

"You're a pretty savvy journalist, Mr. Ryan. I'm sure you must be curious as to why no one has connected the dots between your twenty-four-hour broadcast and the Internet disappearing," the president said.

"Well, I was baffled by that fact, sir," I replied.

"It is because we have made sure that no one mentioned it. You see, Mr. Ryan, almost a third of the literate people on this planet read *Mr. Breeze*, and I'm sure many people, after your return from the dead, are reading it again or for the first time. The last thing we need is for people to start believing we are going to be forced back into the Stone Age," the president said.

"I have spoken to the leaders of every major country over the last twenty-four hours, Mr. Ryan. Being an intelligent man, you are well aware of what would happen if the Internet were to cease to exist," the president told me.

"Yes, sir, I am. The entire financial system around the world would come crumbling down," I answered.

"Yes, that is true, but that may not be the worst of things. As you know, there are some very paranoid leaders out there who believe everything is a plot against them. Some of them possess nuclear weapons, and there is a very strong likelihood that they may launch those weapons if we cannot return things back to normal," the president said.

"How do you think I can help you, Mr. President?" I asked.

"By telling your friend Zack that we surrender. We will do whatever he asks of us, but it is imperative that he return the Internet to an operational status immediately," he said.

It took me a few seconds to process what he'd just said to me. If I'd heard him right, the world just offered to surrender to me.

"Mr. President, with all due respect, I think you and the rest of the world leaders haven't a clue as to what Zack wants. He doesn't want you to surrender, sir, nor does he need you to. He can do whatever he wants to us, and we can't do anything to stop him. You seem to think I am in contact with him. I assure you, I am not. I am trying to save us all, Mr. President, but I will need your help to do that," I said.

I thought I was going to get thrown out on my ass for talking that way to the president, but he didn't seem to be upset. "Let's say I want to help you; what would you have me do?" he asked.

"Mr. President, as you know, I announced that I was going to hold a rally on Wednesday. So far, the National Park Service has not issued me a permit. I need to have that rally, sir. I believe it might be our only chance to show Zack we deserve a chance to survive," I said.

"All right, Mr. Ryan, you will have your rally, but I need something in return. As I told you before, we must have all Internet access restored," the president said.

I picked up the copy of *Mr. Breeze* that was on the table between our chairs and looked through the pages. There was circled text with question marks on many of the pages. "Mr. President, did you make these markings in the book?" I asked.

"Yes, Mr. Ryan, I read the book again before I went to sleep last night," the president replied.

"Well, then you know what Zack thinks of me. I merely served a purpose for him, and he made it very clear that he and I were not friends. I cannot make bargains for him, and I do not speak for him. I am just an ordinary man who is trying my best to do what I think will save all of mankind," I said.

"You should have been a politician, Mr. Ryan. You have a knack for saying what people want to hear, without saying what people want to know," the president told me.

I smiled, not sure if he meant that as a compliment. "Sir, may I suggest that we find a way to keep the financial markets closed until after the rally? I can only hope that Zack will give us some clue of his intentions on Wednesday," I said.

"I will inform the other world leaders about our conversation, and I will include your recommendations. Go make plans for your rally, Mr. Ryan," the president said.

He stood up from his chair, and I followed suit. He reached out his hand to me. "Thank you, Mr. Ryan. I know I never said this before, but thank you for what you did two years ago. I don't think many people realize we are only here because of you," the president said.

"Thank you, sir," I answered and walked toward the door of the oval office. I put my hand on the doorknob and started to open the door, but instead of leaving, I turned around. "Mr. President, there was one thing Zack said that I didn't put in the book. Now I wish I had, but I didn't realize then who he really was," I said.

The president looked up from the papers he was reading at his desk.

"When I asked Zack how one book could possibly change the way people think and act, he told me one book already had, but he said the fools who wrote it had changed his words to fit their needs and that would never happen again. You cannot negotiate with God, sir," I said, and then I left the oval office.

Agent Garcia was waiting for me on the other side of the door. We walked back the same way we came, and he drove me back to the condo and dropped me off. Not a word was spoken the entire trip back.

When I walked into the condo, Missy was, to say the least, excited to see me. She ran over to me and hugged me so tight I thought she was going to break something. "It's OK; you can let go," I said, though it did feel good that she missed me.

"I was worried about you. All this cloak-and-dagger stuff—you never know what could've happened," she said.

155

"Well, one thing that did happen is that we got our permit," I said.

"That's great! So come on, tell me. What did the president say? What's he like? Come on, Michael; tell me what happened," Missy said.

I was never sworn to secrecy, and even if I had been, I think I still would have told Missy what we talked about.

Once I did, she just shook her head. "They really don't understand, do they, Michael?" she asked.

"No, and the worst thing is they seem to think *Mr. Breeze* is a fiction novel I wrote, rather than mankind's final warning," I answered. My phone started to ring, and, as I expected, it was Marty. "Thanks for coming by this morning," I said jokily.

"Yeah, like I was really given a choice," Marty answered.

"We had a nice chat," I said.

"Well, it must have been a very nice chat since your rally permit was just hand-delivered to my office," he said.

"Great, thanks, Marty. I have to run, though; I have a lot of work to do," I said.

"Wait a second. You're not going to tell me what happened? I am your attorney, after all," Marty said.

"Sorry, Marty, but I promised not to reveal any details to anyone," I said lying through my teeth. I didn't have a problem telling Marty; I just didn't want the hour-long conversation it would turn into afterward.

My next call was to Sarah at the *Post*. They owed me, and now was the time for payback. The front page of tomorrow's paper would read "Ryan's Rally Is a Go."

When Missy went to work, she accomplished more in a day and a half than I thought was possible. She organized every detail of the rally, rented the equipment, gave Steve and his men jobs to do, and enlisted Melody, James, and Domenique's help, as well. I didn't think it was even possible, but by Tuesday night, she had everything done. I was exhausted just watching her!

"I cannot believe what you have done in such a short time. Thank you, Missy. I'll see you in the morning. Good night," I said.

Missy smiled. "You see, there is a reason I am here," she said in a joking voice.

"Yes, there are many reasons you are here, and I'm glad for all of them," I replied.

I went into my room and got ready for bed. I had just gotten into bed when I heard a knock on my door. Missy opened the door just wide enough so that I could hear her voice. "Can I come in?" she asked.

"Sure. Is there something wrong?" I replied.

Missy walked into my bedroom and sat down on the edge of the bed. "I am just feeling a little nervous about tomorrow, and I was wondering if I could sleep—and I mean only sleep—next to you tonight," she said.

"Of course you can, and believe me, I am nervous about tomorrow too," I said.

Missy jumped off the bed and ran out of the bedroom. She returned with two additional pillows in her hands. "I like a lot of pillows," she said. Missy arranged her four pillows the way she wanted them and then got into the bed with me. "Good night, Michael," she said.

"Good night, Missy," I replied.

It had been a long time since I had slept with anyone in my bed. I wasn't sure how well I would sleep, but it turned out I went right to sleep.

When I woke up the next morning, Missy was still sound asleep, lying there next to me.

I wasn't sure whether it was her perfume or what she used on her hair that I was smelling, but it smelled wonderful. *I could get used to waking up like this,* I thought to myself. I looked over at the clock. It was just about six, and we needed to be at the Mall by eight, so I tried my best to get out of bed quietly.

"I'm awake," Missy said.

"I'm sorry; I hope I didn't wake you," I told her.

"No, you didn't wake me, and thank you for letting me sleep here last night," she said, getting up. "I'm going to shower. We need to leave soon," she said, walking out of the bedroom.

I could not take my eyes off of her as she got out of bed and walked away. I was just mesmerized by her beauty and how gracefully she moved. I guess with everything that had happened, I had not really noticed how truly amazing she was. I would not make that mistake again.

I finally got up and showered, shaved, and dressed. When I was done, I went into the kitchen, made coffee, and had a banana for my breakfast. I wasn't really hungry, but I knew I needed to eat something. Just as I was pouring my coffee, I heard a knock at the front door. I looked through the peephole. It was Steve Reton. I opened the door and let him in. "Come on in, Steve; can I get you a cup of coffee?" I asked as I opened the door.

"No, thanks; I'm fine," Steve answered.

"Missy is still getting ready. When do you think we should leave?" I asked.

"The sooner, the better, Michael. We will have a police escort to the Mall, and they are already outside on the street waiting for us," Steve said.

"OK, just let me grab a yogurt, and I'm ready," Missy said walking into the kitchen.

Chapter Eleven

When we got down to the street, there were police cars everywhere. Charlie was standing next to the limo with his hand on the opened rear door. "Good morning," he said.

"Good Morning, Michael, Missy," Charlie said looking over to Missy.

"This is some circus, Charlie," I said looking out at the thirty-plus police cars within my sight. "After a forty-foot dog, this doesn't seem all that strange to me," Charlie answered as we climbed into the limo and he closed the door. I laughed to myself, but I did wonder where Rover was. I was pretty sure he was going to make an appearance this morning, but it seemed I was wrong. With a small army of police cars as our escort, we had little trouble with traffic and we arrived at the Mall before 8:00 a.m.

The area was roped off, and they had called on the National Guard to assist with security and crowd control. We were directed to an area behind a large stage that had been constructed for the rally. There were two large RVs parked in back, as well as five large tents. Charlie parked the limo next to one of the RVs.

"Let me see what's going on. The rest of you, please stay here," Steve said. He came back a few minutes later. "They want us to stay in the trailers until noon," he said.

159

"All right," I said, and we got out of the limo. Steve pointed to the trailer we would use, and Missy and I and the Williams went inside. Steve and his men went into the other. Marty was there waiting inside the trailer for me.

"Wow, you're up early," I said. Marty did not look very happy to be there.

"Can we talk in private?" he asked.

"I have no secrets from anyone here, Marty," I answered. Marty pointed to Domenique. "OK, let's go back into the bedroom of this thing," I said tapping Missy's arm. It was cramped, but the three of us were able to fit inside and close the door.

"What did you promise the president, Michael?" Marty asked.

"I didn't promise the president anything, Marty. In fact, I told him he couldn't make deals with God," I said.

"Well, it seems he thought if they let you go ahead and have your little rally, then your friend would bring back the Internet," Marty told me.

"What! You're fucking kidding me, right?" I said with anger coming through in my voice. Marty shook his head no. "Never trust a politician. So they still think I can just yell up into the sky and say, 'Zack, do this' or 'Zack, do that,'" I said incredulously.

"So, why are you here, Marty?" Missy asked, being more level-headed than I was at the moment.

"I am here because I think that if the Internet doesn't go back on by noon and anything goes wrong here, they are going to come down hard on you, Michael," Marty said.

"Thanks, Marty. Missy, do me a favor; go find Steve and bring him back here," I asked.

Missy got up and opened the door. Steve was standing out there waiting for us. I walked out of the bedroom and gathered everyone together. I felt that the Williams needed to know what was going on.

I told them all about my being brought to the White House and my conversation with the president, as well as what Marty had just told me. "Look, Michael, as your attorney, I advise you not to go out there unless you are sure that what they want to happen will. As your friend, though, I say screw them all and go out there and do what you believe in," Marty said.

"We are with you, Michael," James and Melody said in unison.

"Me too," Domenique added.

I looked over at Steve. "You've done enough, Steve. If something goes wrong, they could use it to fire you and your men. After all, you are police officers. I think it's time for you and your men to leave the rest of this to us," I said.

"Are you sure, Michael?" Steve asked.

"Yes, Steve, I am sure. I want to thank you for everything you and your men did, but you need to go home," I said, shaking his hand.

"Good luck, Michael," Steve said, and he left the RV.

"That was a pretty noble thing to do, Michael. You really aren't the same man I used to know.

If it's all right with you, I'd like to stick around. I read *Mr. Breeze* again last night. I think I understand what you're trying to accomplish, and I'd like to help," Marty said.

"Thanks, Marty, but I have a feeling you may be more of a help back at your office arranging for my bail and my defense, once I'm arrested," I said.

Marty looked over at Missy and the Williams. "You're probably right. Please be careful out there, all of you," Marty said giving me a quick hug before he left the RV.

"Michael, I'm going to take the girls over to the food tent I spotted when we drove in," James said. I wasn't sure whether they were hungry or if he knew I needed to talk to Missy alone.

"What's wrong?" Missy asked as soon as they left the RV.

"I guess I thought he would have shown himself by now, Missy, or at least Rover. What the fuck am I doing here?" I said with an anxious voice.

"Michael, calm down; you know he is watching you," Missy said, trying her best to urge me on.

"Did you see the signs people had out there? 'Hang the Devil,' 'Save the Whales,' 'Ryan Is Dyin',' 'Burn Mr. Breeze'—these are the fools I am trying to save. For what, Missy? For what?" I asked.

"They aren't all bad, Michael, and I know you believe in what you are doing, so what's really bothering you?" Missy asked.

"Yeah, I guess you're right. We do need to save the whales," I said with a smile. I knew I needed to come clean with her.

"You know, Missy, I have come a long way in the last two years, and like the song says, 'what a long strange trip it's been.' But what I have come to understand does not sit with what I want," I said.

Missy gave me one of those "what are you talking about" looks.

"I now know that Zack wants us to believe, not in him, but in ourselves. He wants us to look inside for our own strength and to turn to each other for guidance and learn to live as one people. There is a part of me that wants his approval. I don't know; maybe it's a product of my childhood, but I guess it would be nice if he gave me a pat on the back or something," I said.

"So, you want an atta boy from God, Michael?" Missy asked, trying not to laugh. I guess it was kind of silly if you looked at that way. I began to laugh, and Missy joined in.

"There is one thing you need to promise me, though," I said, and I finished laughing.

"And what is that?" Missy asked.

"I'm pretty sure we've seen the last of the Internet, and I am almost positive that I am going to get arrested for something, either during or after this rally. What you need to promise me is that you will try to not get yourself arrested and also help Marty get me out when I do," I said.

"OK, I promise," Missy answered.

Missy went outside to the food tent and brought back a variety of stuff for the two of us. She had hired a catering company as part of the preparations she had made. I turned on the TV to see what kind of coverage we were getting. I was pleased to see that there were a few parts of the world that were also holding their own rallies. The main focus of the reports were here in DC, where the crowd size was estimated at close to one million people.

Of course, there was also mention of the still mysterious cause of the outage of the Internet and how the global financial markets would remain closed today. Well, at least the president had heard what I said about that. I watched as the news cameras showed various parts of the crowd I was soon to stand before. It seemed by the signs and the chants coming from the people that there was about a fifty-fifty spilt—half here supported what Zack wanted from us, and the other half wanted to see me dead.

I had asked people to bring copies of Mr. Breeze with them, and many people did, but there were also those who were shown on film burning copies of the book in trash cans and chanting, "Down with the devil! Ryan is dying!"

I heard a knock at the door of the RV. Missy must have, as well, and she went to see who it was. I saw a man in uniform step inside the RV. "Good morning," I said.

"Mr. Ryan, my name is Colonel Lanza, and I am in command of the National Guardsmen who are here to help keep things under control." Colonel Lanza was tall and lean with dark brown hair, and I guessed he was in his early forties. He struck me as a "get right to the point" type of guy, so I was going to give him the opportunity to do just that.

"What can I do for you, Colonel?" I asked.

"You can get back in that limo out there and go home, Mr. Ryan. There are close to a million people out there, many of whom would probably like to see you dead, and I cannot guarantee either your safety or the safety of the people in this crowd if you go out there," he said.

"I am sorry, Colonel, but I cannot do that. I must go out there and address the crowd," I replied.

"Mr. Ryan, I don't know whether you are brave, determined, selfish, or just a fool, but my direct orders from the president prohibit me from stopping this rally. It appears only you can make that call, so I appeal to you once again to please reconsider your decision," Colonel Lanza said.

"Colonel, I am probably a little bit of everything you just mentioned. Just be aware of what will happen if I don't go out there. It will be far worse than what will happen if I do," I replied.

I didn't know for sure what would happen if I didn't go on the stage and address the crowd, but I had made my decision and I had had enough of the colonel's attempt to frighten everyone. "As you wish," the colonel said, and he made his way out of the RV.

"James, Melody, I want you to get inside the limo when I go out to address the crowd, and if anything goes wrong, get Charlie to help you get out of here," I said. "Missy, I really think it would be best if you let me go on that stage alone. I don't want to be responsible for anything that might happen to you. After all, you are all Kim has left," I told her, hoping that using her daughter might make her listen.

Missy looked at me for a moment. "All right, Michael, but I am standing right next to the stage. I am not going in the limo," she said.

"Fine, but please try to stay out of sight," I said.

It was ten minutes before noon when we left the RV. James and Melody wished me luck, and Domenique gave me a big hug before they got into the limo. "Charlie, if anything goes wrong here, make sure you get them and Missy out of here as fast as you can," I said.

Charlie got out of the limo and stood in front of me. "It has been an honor to know you, Mr. Ryan. Good luck today," he said and put his hand out to me.

"Thanks, Charlie," I said shaking his hand.

Missy and I walked toward the stage, stopping at the steps. "You stay here please, Missy. For once, do what I ask," I said.

"You are worried about me?" she asked.

"Yes, I am. I have gotten kind of used to having you around," I said.

"Well, I have gotten used to being around too, and I think I'll keep being around," she said. She put her arms around me and kissed me. "Go save the world, Michael," she said, releasing me from her arms.

"I'll do my best," I said with a smile, as I climbed the steps to the stage.

When I walked up onto the stage, there was nothing there but a stand with a microphone attached to it. I looked out onto a huge sea of people. At first, they didn't even notice I was there. I walked up to the microphone. "Good afternoon, and thank you all for being here," I said.

For a moment, there was silence in the crowd, and then all you could hear were cheers and the chants about my death and about the devil. There was a temporary barricade set up so no one could get any closer than about twenty feet from the stage, and there were dozens of police officers standing between the stage and the barrier.

I saw one man moving through the crowd, and he screamed, "Die, you devil worshipper," before he threw what looked like a grenade at the stage. When the object reached the edge of the stage, it was sucked into some sort of invisible shield and vanished. Suddenly, there was silence again. The man who threw the object was being beaten by others in the crowd. "Please, leave him alone. We are not here for violence," I ordered. They stopped beating on him.

Missy saw what had happened and, as usual, did not listen to me. She was now up on the stage with me. I smiled at her but gave her one of my "why can't you listen" looks.

"I have come here today, not as an American, not as a white male, and not as someone who does not believe in any of your religions. I come to you as a human being, because we are all human beings and we share this planet together; it is time we learned to live on it together in peace." There was a huge roar from the crowd. The cheers were so loud they drowned out the angry chanters.

"We must learn to respect each other as equals. We must learn to forget our petty differences and to understand that the only way we are going to survive is to do it together. Like it or not, people, we have met our maker and his patience with us has expired."

I could see large groups of people carrying "Ryan Is Dyin'" signs coming up through the crowd. They started hitting people as they walked through the crowd. Some had what looked like small bats, and they smashed people's arms as they held up copies of *Mr. Breeze.*

It appeared that their plan to kill me had failed, so now they were intent on starting a riot. And that was exactly what they did. People were beating on each other everywhere. They were throwing things at the police and the National Guard. It was a total disaster. The police rushed up on the stage, knocked me down, pulled my hands behind my back, and handcuffed me. Of course, Missy did not listen to what I said earlier, and she grabbed at the police officers and screamed at them to stop trying to hurt me. I was not resisting, and they, of course, arrested her too.

When they took us off the stage, I noticed the limo was gone. I was glad Charlie had gotten the Williams to safety.

They separated Missy and me, and I was taken in and charged with inciting a riot. I spent the remainder of the day in a holding cell, and then I was moved to another cell that had a small and very uncomfortable bed. The next morning, the guards brought me breakfast. They put me in a bulletproof vest, handcuffed my wrists and ankles, and took me out of the cell, and then I was driven to the courthouse. I was taken in through a side entrance; there were guards everywhere.

It wasn't easy to walk handcuffed. A weird kind of penguin walk was all that I could manage. I was brought into the courtroom, and I saw Missy was already there with Marty sitting next to her. I was seated in the chair on the end, closest to the aisle. "Are you OK?" I asked Missy.

"I'm fine. You?" she asked.

"I'm good, but this is a bullshit charge," I said.

"I told you they would come after you if the Internet didn't go back on," Marty said.

"Can you get us out of here?" I asked.

"Missy, for you, it shouldn't be a problem. For you, Michael, that might be more difficult. I think they want to deny you bail and hold you until your buddy turns the lights back on," Marty said.

The judge walked in, and we all rose. His name was the Honorable Richard Leonard. He was probably in his early sixties, and he didn't look like he was too pleased to be there. I looked around the courtroom and counted fifteen armed guards. In the back row, I saw James, Melody, and Domenique.

"Your Honor, I am Marty Charles. I represent Mr. Ryan and Ms. Franzone. I would like to ask the court to drop all charges against my clients," Marty said.

"Sit down, Mr. Charles. In my courtroom, I decide when you get to speak," Judge Leonard said banging his gavel. The doors to the courtroom burst open, and Rover came walking in. The guards reached for their guns, and it would turn out to be the last thing they ever did as they instantly fell to the floor. Rover looked at the judge, and he ran out of the courtroom. I looked around at the rest of the courtroom, and everyone seemed to be frozen in their seats. Besides Missy, Marty, and me, only James, Melody, and Domenique seemed able to move.

Rover stopped when he got to the table where Missy and I were sitting. He looked at the chains, and they vanished. Then he turned and looked toward the door of the courtroom. Zack came walking in. Missy grabbed my wrist and squeezed it. Zack raised his arm slightly, and Kim came running into the courtroom. Missy let go of my wrist and ran over to her. She hugged her and lifted her off the ground.

Zack looked over and saw the Williams. Domenique walked over and stood in right front of him. "I knew I'd see you again," she said.

"You are a brave and wise little girl," Zack told her, and he patted her on the head.

I walked over to Zack. "Hello, Zack, I guess things did not work out exactly like I planned," I said.

"Well, Michael, that remains to be seen. I'm afraid the time has come. You will be coming with me. Rover will take the others with him," Zack said.

"Where are we going, Zack?" I asked, somehow knowing I wouldn't get an answer.

Missy ran over to me and put her arms around my neck. There were tears in her eyes. "Thank you, Michael. You gave me a reason to want to feel again," she whispered in my ear.

My eyes started to tear up as well. "You did the same for me, and you also made me realize what I was meant to do and who I was meant to be," I told her.

Zack just stood there, unaffected by our emotional moment. "Michael, thank you for trying," Melody Williams said before she quickly disappeared along with James, Domenique, Missy, and Kim. I had no idea where Rover had taken them.

"May I have a minute to say good-bye to someone?" I asked.

Zack nodded in approval, and I walked over to Marty. "I know you never believed in all this, Marty, but I want to thank you for everything you did for me. Good-bye," I said holding out my hand. Marty took my hand and just looked at me. I didn't think he knew what to say or if he realized what was about to happen.

The next thing I knew, I was in a room or a hallway or something. It seemed to have no shape, and it was endless. Zack was standing a few feet from me. "It is time, Zack. Are you here to make good on your promise to destroy us all?" I asked.

"No, Michael, I am not going to destroy you," Zack said.

"Then what?" I asked.

"This morning, I took away your currency. Your world is now as financially bankrupt as it is emotionally," Zack said.

"What do you mean?" I asked.

"Money. Michael, it is all gone. The precious metals—everything is gone. Every person and every entity is now without currency," Zack said. "I warned you a long time ago to beware of money and what it would do to your society, but you didn't listen. Instead, you built a world that worshipped it. You put those with great wealth above others, foolishly thinking that those who had managed to make more money had made a success of their lives," Zack said.

"So, you will watch what transpires from here, Michael. I will not destroy you; you will destroy yourselves. Very soon, one of your leaders will launch their country's entire arsenal of destructive weapons, and then there will be retaliation launches. In a very short time, no one will be left alive," Zack said.

"Zack, please, you can stop this. Show them your power; show them who you really are. I know I can get them to listen to me if you do. We can change, Zack. We can," I begged him.

"Michael, those of great power have no reason to constantly show it. That task is left to those with great fear, like those you live among," Zack said.

I had no fucking idea what that meant, but I knew I was running out of time, and then it hit me.

"You knew I would fail, didn't you? The book you made me write, this whole thing was what? A game for you? I believe in myself, Zack, and I believe in mankind. No, we aren't perfect, but we have the capacity to change. We are your children, are we not? So if you must punish us, do it. But please, there are so many innocent people out there who will die if you allow this to happen. I beg you; please do something to stop it. If you truly need to punish someone, then I offer myself to you. I will take whatever punishment you wish if it will spare just some of those who have done nothing other than to exist," I said.

Zack just looked at me. I could see he was not going to change his mind. Our time had come. I started to think about what I could have done differently in my life. I had many regrets. I guessed most people did though. As I stood there next to our creator, I couldn't help but wonder whether this was all just a repeat for him. Was this the first time he would destroy us or the tenth, and would there be another me standing here ten thousand years from now?

"Will you allow me to see Missy and her daughter one last time?" I asked.

Zack did not answer my question; suddenly, many images filled the room, images of our earth. He was right. I saw the missiles launching. At first, they were from only one location, but, in what seemed like seconds later, they were coming from everywhere. I fell to my knees as I watched the mushroom clouds envelope the planet.

My immediate thoughts were of Missy and Kim, and then I started to cry. I cried for people I had known and for so many others I'd never even met. I knew I would soon be joining them; I just didn't know when. I looked up at Zack. I began to feel tired, and then everything went blank.

Epilogue

Day One

I woke up feeling a little groggy. I found myself lying in a bed. *Wait a second,* I thought. *How did I wake up, and where the fuck am I?* I sat up in the bed, and the first thing I noticed was how fresh and clean the air smelled. I look down on the floor, and there was Rover sleeping peacefully.

He woke up, stood, and looked at me. *"Don't be nervous, Michael; it is me, Rover,"* I heard in my head as there was no sound coming to my ears.

"Oh shit, this is really fucked up. Where am I, Rover? Where is Zack?" I asked.

"Get dressed, and come with me, Michael," I heard in my head.

I put on my clothes and walked out of the bedroom. Missy was standing in the kitchen drinking a glass of juice. "Good morning, sleepyhead," she said coming over. She kissed me on the cheek.

"Good morning," I responded still not sure of what was going on.

"I am going over to the hospital to check on things. I will see you for dinner, my sleepy husband," she said as she walked out of the room.

173

"All right, Rover, I am about to freak out here. She thinks we're married! What is going on?"

Just then, two boys came running into the house. "Hi, Dad," one of them said as he ran by me.

I looked at him; he looked just like a mini me, but gazing at him brought back an image I had of my mother. It was her; he looked like her. The other boy came up and hugged me.

"Morning, Dad," he said and then ran off. I was starting to feel dizzy, and I thought I was going to pass out when Rover put his paw on my foot. Suddenly, I felt stable again.

"*Follow me, Michael,*" Rover told me. I followed him outside, and I was amazed at what I saw. We were in some sort of settlement where the houses all looked alike. People were outside playing, and I could hear the laughter of both children and adults. I walked with Rover, and I saw people I recognized: James and Melody Williams, Nancy, Marty, Missy's sister Ann, and Steve Reton. They all said good morning to me, in fact, everyone said good morning to me and they all knew my name.

It was unsettling at first, but the longer I walked around with Rover, the more I felt at home.

"Good Morning, Michael," a young woman said to me.

It took me a moment to remember, but it was Janice, the woman Zack had saved in San Francisco two years ago. However, she was forty years younger than the last time I saw her. I kept looking around. I saw Kim and Domenique playing together, laughing and smiling.

Rover led me through the little town. I didn't see any stores, restaurants, gas stations, or anything that I would have thought was necessary to sustain human existence.

"Good Morning, Michael," Zack said, appearing out of nowhere.

I must have had quite a look on my face when he saw me. "Don't worry; all of your questions will be answered. Walk with me," he ordered.

"Where am I? Where is this place?" I asked.

"This is Earth, Michael, and you and the fifteen hundred adults and the three thousand children that are here are all that is left of the human race," Zack told me.

"Missy thinks she is my wife and those boys—they called me 'Dad,' and they look like me. How can this be?" I asked.

"Missy is your wife, Michael. And those boys, Taylor and Jake, they are your sons. I created them in your image. You see, you are the only one here who remembers anything about what was," Zack told me.

I was starting to feel a little wobbly again, and Zack reached out his hand and touched my shoulder steadying me, but his touch also cleared my mind of the fog I had felt since I woke up. "Why, Zack? Why this?" I asked.

"You are all of my creation, Michael. My children, if you prefer to use that term. I allowed mankind to go astray and so it is time to start over. This time, things will be different," Zack said.

"Why will it be different this time?" I asked.

Zack didn't answer my question. Instead, we just walked until we came upon a pedestal that was about five feet tall stuck into the ground. We stopped in front of it, and both Zack and Rover looked at me. "Put your hand on it, Michael," Zack said.

I placed my hand on top of the pedestal, and the next thing I knew we were all inside a huge building. It was like a giant warehouse, and it seemed to go on forever.

"Here is what your mankind has produced, Michael. Here is your literature, your art, your history, and even your music," Zack said and he

175

pointed to an area labeled "Grateful Dead." It was amazing! Everything that our world had produced was now behind labels. "You can have access to this place anytime you wish, Michael. All you need to do is go to the entry point as you did today. As you can see, there are exit points throughout this area," Zack said. I could see the pedestals as I looked in every direction. There seemed to be no end to this structure.

"How about Missy and the others? Can I share this place with them?" I asked.

"No, Michael. For now, you will be the only one who will be allowed to access this area. You see, aside from removing all memories, I have given each of the others a certain set of skills that will be needed to enhance this new world. Missy is now a doctor, and she has also been given a wonderful singing voice and the ability to sense others' emotions. The others are artists, builders, teachers, and musicians. They all have special talents, Michael," Zack said.

"What is my talent, Zack?" I asked.

Zack looked at me and smiled. I thought he even started to laugh. "You still do not understand, do you, Michael?"

"Understand what, Zack? What am I missing?" I replied.

"This has been all about you from the beginning," Zack said.

"Me? No, Zack, I don't understand. What do you mean?" I asked.

"Michael, I told you that I have watched over you your entire life. What I did not tell you is that I have been testing you, as well. You were born with no faith, but over time, you became more open to believing. When you did decide to believe, you chose to believe in yourself and mankind instead of believing in me. You see, believing in yourselves is all I have ever wanted for my children.

"My teachings were designed to do one thing—to show you how to live. Your religions were made up to control and to separate people, and no human being I had ever come across understood that better than you," Zack said.

I stood there processing everything I had just heard, still not sure I completely understood. "We can talk about sharing this with the others in a few thousand years from now, Michael," Zack said. Now, that statement got my attention.

"A few thousand years, Zack? Did I hear that right? You and I will be talking in a few thousand years?" I asked.

"Yes, Michael, you and Missy will become the guides for all who will follow you. You will help those who are here now and those who will come later to avoid making the same mistakes again. You will teach them what you have learned. You will not age, Michael, nor will Missy. Your children and their children will help build a new world where there are only equals. No one will be put above anyone ever again."

"For now, I will provide everything you need: food, shelter, all the things necessary to survive. Rover will be your constant companion; in fact, he asked me if I would allow him to stay with you. He has grown quite attached to you, Michael. There will be no need for wars. You see, humans are no longer capable of violence and the cruelty that controlled so much of your world is gone as well. I know this all seems overwhelming to you right now, but in time, you will understand your purpose and you will embrace it with the same passion that you did with everything else you did in your life. Go, my son. Make me a proud father," Zack said.

"So, all of what you did while you were with me was what, Zack? A test for me? You intended this all along. There never was a chance of our civilization surviving, was there?" I asked with anger in my voice.

"You forget your place, Michael, but I will forgive you this time. I warned mankind what the consequences would be if they were unable to change. And yes, Michael, everything you have ever done in your life has been a test," Zack answered.

177

The next thing I knew, Rover and I were walking down the street where my home was located. I still did not know how many people I knew had survived or who the fifteen hundred adults Zack chose to survive were. I guess I would find out soon enough.

When we got to the house, Kim, Taylor, and Jake were playing on the front yard along with a few other children. *"Do you mind?"* I heard Rover's thoughts in my head. This was going to take time to get used to, having him in my head.

"Sure, go play. Have fun," I said to Rover, and he ran over and began playing with the children. He looked like any normal dog rolling around on the grass.

I sat down on a bench on the front lawn and just watched all of them play. This really was a paradise, and I was going to live in it for…I guess only Zack knew how long. Someday, maybe I would tell Missy, but not for a long time. She deserved to be happy. In the end, Zack was right. We had built a world that was bound to collapse, sooner or later. We had become ruled, not by our hearts or even our minds, but by our wallets.

Missy came out of the house and began to play with the children and Rover on the front lawn. They all seemed so happy. Maybe it was best that they never knew the truth—that almost everyone and everything they ever knew was gone. I thought about what had just happened and what Zack was asking of me.

I had no idea why Zack thought I was up to this task, and the only one I could confide in about all of this was a dog. Boy, was I in a whole shitload of trouble! I felt something in my back pocket. I took it out and unfolded it. It was a letter from Zack.

I have given the human race another chance, Michael, and I have given them you as their guide. I have chosen Missy for you. She will help you maintain your humanity as the years go by. You asked me what your special talent was. It is your passion, the passion you have shown your whole life to find the truth in everything and to do what is right, no matter what the cost. I am aware of the pain you feel for all of those who were lost, but you must try to look ahead and find the strength to do what is needed. Do not let mankind make the same mistakes again, Michael. Make sure my children are taught well. You think of yourself as an ordinary human, Michael. Well, always remember this: all humans are ordinary until they do something extraordinary.